Left, Right and Centre

reflections on composers
and composing

by
GEOFFREY BUSH

THAMES PUBLISHING
14 Barlby Road   London W10 6AR

Contents

ALSO BY GEOFFREY BUSH

Musical Creation and the Listener (London: Frederick Muller. New York: Hawthorn Books, Inc.).

Chapters on Song and Chamber Music in *The Athlone History of British Music, V: The Romantic Age* (Athlone Press).

With Edmund Crispin
> *Who killed Baker?* included in *Fen Country* (Gollancz), *Best Detective Stories* (Faber), *Modern Short Stories 1940–80* (Everyman: Dent).

With John Elliot
> *Space:* a revue for television (BBC, 1958).
> *Never die:* a play for television (BBC, 1960).

PART I

1. Left, right and centre

Ever since the Furies were named 'the Kindly Ones' by the Ancient Greeks, men have used words to disguise the truth as much as to reveal it. That squid-like creature, the politician in power, is particularly adept at concealing his objectives behind a cloud of ink. Take the word 'defence'. This appears an acceptable concept to many people because it sounds essentially pacific. What lies concealed is the determination to resort to genocide in the event of a conflict — or even, by 'pre-emptive strike', *before* a conflict. (To argue that the nuclear deterrent is 'only a threat' is disingenuous. No empty bluff can constitute an effective threat.) Or again, take the expression 'the free world'. Two thirds of the so-called free world are ruled by military dictatorships whose reliance on imprisonment, torture and assassination as a means of eliminating their opponents would have ensured them a warm welcome at the court of Ghengis Khan. The inhabitants of the remaining third are seldom at liberty to control the policy of their rulers — consider, in our own country, the cynical disregard of conference decisions by party leaders. The principal freedom they possess is the right of unavailing complaint.

Where 'vital interests are at stake' (another delightfully deceptive phrase) musicians have been quick to follow the politicians' example. It often happens that a critic invests, so to speak, his spiritual capital in a particular aesthetic movement or in one particular composer. To prevent his investment depreciating, emotive words often have to be pressed into service. In the past both Wagner and Debussy had their unscrupulous camp-followers; more recently the Second Viennese School has suffered from the same undesirable partisanship. It is not enough that these three composers were leading figures in the Expressionist movement, perhaps the most far-reaching artistic development of the 20th century; it must also be claimed on their behalf that they were all things to all men. Hence the application of the words 'tuneful' and 'comic' to certain aspects of their music.

The value of the word 'tune' lies in its associations; hearing it, the mind instantly conjures up the memorable, and singable, inspirations of a Purcell, a Verdi or a Gershwin. But if there is one thing missing from the mainstream of music in recent years it is a tune. Melody — and indeed harmony and rhythm in the traditional sense — has had to yield pride of place to colour and texture in avant-garde circles.

Pitch has been demoted. But by applying the word 'tune', with all its resonances, either to a line that resembles a fever patient's temperature chart or to a motif so brief that it can be immediately re-incarnated as a single chord, it is possible to suggest that music today has exactly the same kind of appeal as the music of the past; and that it has been able to acquire new attractions in the way of timbre without sacrificing any of the elements which are central to the work of a truly universal composer like Mozart.

The word 'comic' has similar implications. It conjures up visions of Rossini, of Sullivan, of Offenbach, and of the unforced laughter which is the characteristic audience response. Nothing could be further from the spirit of Expressionism. There can of course be irony and satire in Expressionist music, just as there are in the drawings of George Grosz and the stage lampoons of Berthold Brecht. The scene in *Wozzeck* where the doctor congratulates the captain on his impending paralysis because of the marvellous experiments which will then be carried out on him is, in its black way, exceedingly funny. But *comic*, no.

There are technical as well as psychological reasons for this, not surprisingly; for what a great composer has to say is inextricably bound up with how he tries to say it.

Donald Grout has summarised the favourite themes of Expressionism as 'fears, tensions, anxieties and the irrational dictates of the sub-conscious', and these are best expressed in fully chromatic music with a high proportion of discord. No wonder Schoenberg found it necessary to 'liberate the dissonance'. Unfortunately, to liberate the dissonance is to enslave the consonance; and without consonance there can be no release from tension and without release from tension there cannot be (in any real sense) comic music. But, the True Believer replies, there can be *degrees* of dissonance; in a totally dissonant situation a weak discord can perform the function of a concord. The weight of this argument can be tested by a small practical experiment. Next time a friend tells you that he is suffering from an ordinary headache, point out that since he has neither a migraine nor a nervous breakdown he is in every respect enjoying perfect health. His reaction may be instructive.

It could be argued that the first two words of my title are equally open to misconstruction; but unlike Bret Harte's Heathen Chinee I have not used 'the same with intent to deceive'. In politics, 'left' and 'right' are generally used to mark the distinction between revolutionary and reactionary societies, and so may justifiably be applied to two sections of a book devoted respectively to Soviet and English music. In order to avoid any suggestion that the one system is less conservative than the other, I have deliberately refrained from specifying which description is applicable to which. (One may well ask, however, whether anything could be more reactionary than a once idealistic régime which has now abandoned all progress towards a juster society in order to maintain itself indefinitely in power.) Above all, no link is implied between an innovatory approach to art and a revolutionary attitude to politics. It is in fact the fearsome dilemma of composers like Nono and Henze that their music would be the first to be proscribed if people's democracies of the kind they advocate came into power all over Europe.

In the first paragraph of his book *My childhood*, Carl Nielsen takes to task those occasional authors 'who apologise for presuming to write about themselves'. In Nielsen's view this attitude is quite wrong: 'If man, as it is said, is the supreme creation and the study of mankind the most important and interesting that we know, then clearly we cannot have enough information about one man or many.' This must serve as my excuse for devoting the last third of the book to my own concerns. In defence of my appropriation of the word 'centre' to define my position, I would advance my membership of such middle-of-the-road organisations as the British Labour Party and the Anglican church, coupled with the information recently given to my wife by an outfitter (on receipt of my order for a made-to-measure suit): 'Madam, your husband is a medium man'.

The centre is not necessarily the safest place to occupy; it has been well said that those who walk in the middle of the road are the likeliest to be run over. In my experience, professionals find my music ridiculously simple and amateurs appallingly difficult, making either an élitist or a popular audience equally out of the question. Fortunately for my peace of mind there is nothing whatever to be done about it; in Mahler's words 'we do not compose, we are composed'. To every creative artist certain things are given to say which he must express to the utmost of his ability; he cannot express what is given to other people. This is not to advocate a mind closed to new ideas. On the contrary, a composer should try to learn from everything that is going on around him. But ideas should not be adopted, as so often today, *solely* because they are new. Imitation of a currently acceptable model like Penderecki is, in essence, no different from the imitation of an unacceptable one like Edmund Rubbra. Both produce second-hand music. If anything, the former is more risky; as Lady Markby warned in Oscar Wilde's *An ideal husband*: 'Nothing is so dangerous as being too modern; one is apt to grow old-fashioned quite suddenly'.

The pressures on young composers to conform have never been as great as they are today; my generation were fortunate to grow up at a time when the centre was not yet forbidden ground.

2. Exchange visit

'Soviet Russia' and 'Soviet music' are good examples of terms which are calculated to confuse rather than to clarify.

The confusion resulting from the former is two-fold. In the first place, the adjective 'Soviet' implies something quite different from 'Tsarist' Russia. True, since 1917 there have been great changes, some (mass education, for example) demonstrably for the better; but many of the abuses for which the Soviet Government is so rightly castigated were inherited directly from the Tsars: inefficient bureaucracy, an all-too-efficient secret police, penal labour camps and suffocating censorship. (It is a shock to discover, on reading Tolstoy's biography for the first time, how much of his work, like that of Solzhenitsyn, had to be circulated in *samizdat*.) Secondly, the phrase implies that Russia is a unified country, whereas it is in fact a loose-knit confederation of many different peoples — centrally governed, admittedly — each with their own culture, customs, cuisine, language and (in some cases) alphabet.

In the same way the term 'Soviet music' leads one to suppose that the ruling party has always adopted a single, undeviating attitude towards composers and their work; whereas during the past 60 years four quite different approaches can be discerned. In the early days of the Revolution, experiment was felt to be quite compatible with Communist thinking. Kandinsky was painting abstracts, Mayakovsky was writing *The Bedbug* and Shostakovitch was composing *The Nose*. By 1936, however, Kandinsky had long since left, Mayakovsky had committed suicide, and the taming of Shostakovitch had begun. The ensuing Stalinist tyranny reached a climax in 1948 at the Composers' Congress presided over by the repulsive Zhdanov, when all the forward-looking composers — most notably Khatachurian, Prokofiev and Shostakovitch — were publicly disgraced. Fortunately all bad things come to an end; in 1953 Stalin died and the Khruschev thaw began. The resolutions of the 1948 congress were, effectively, rescinded, Solzhenitsyn's *One day in the life of Ivan Denisovitch* was published in *Novy Mir*, and compositions such as Shostakovitch's 4th Symphony and 1st Violin Concerto, which had been buried in a drawer, were triumphantly disinterred. The fourth period in this lightning summary of Soviet musical history began in 1964 with the fall of Khruschev. An immediate deterioration followed; but if Brezhnev's régime has failed to be as flexible as that of his predecessor at its best, it has mercifully proved less rigorous than Stalin's at its worst.

One corrective for these misunderstandings is a trip to Russia; and in 1964 I had the good fortune to be chosen, with John Gardner, to represent the Composers' Guild of Great Britain on a three-week exchange visit to the Union of Soviet Composers. It may reasonably be objected that three weeks is too short a period to permit of the formation of opinions of any value, particularly as delegates see only what has been expressly passed fit for their consumption. This is perfectly true; but in our case two unusual factors worked to our advantage. Firstly, we had already made personal contact with a number of Russian composers and writers on music who had visited England under the exchange system, so that we were not starting from scratch. Secondly, we had as our interpreter a young physics student who worked during his vacations as a translator in one or other of the languages he had learnt from study courses on the radio. He was, to say the least, no admirer of the régime, and his comments plus — something less easily defined but even more instructive — his attitudes, gave us a perspective on what we were shown which would have surprised (and probably alarmed) our official hosts.

We began by travelling across Europe by train. Our coach was a Russian one, complete with samovar at the end of the corridor from which hot drinks could be made at any time of day or night. At each stage of the journey we were hauled by a different locomotive; through Holland we were part of a Dutch train, through Poland a Polish one, with restaurant cars to match. On arrival at the Soviet frontier our coach was hoisted upwards by crane while the narrow-gauge bogies of the European system were wheeled away and wide-gauge Russian ones (which make for smoother travelling) substituted. Including the channel crossing the journey lasted two and a half days; what brought the enormous size of Russia home to us was the fact that that we should have needed another five days to cross Siberia and reach the country's Eastern border. (Later we also learnt that the distance from north to south was greater than from London to Moscow.) Except for the principal cities the satellite countries through which we passed seemed undeveloped and poverty-stricken compared with our own — and, indeed, compared with Russia itself. East Germany was perhaps an exception; but what it lacked in poverty it amply made up for in drabness.

Our first two destinations were Moscow and Leningrad, twin musical capitals of Soviet Russia; and there we began to appreciate for the first time the resources and authority of the Composers' Union. We had sent

10

to them in advance of our arrival a varied assortment of our music —
pieces for string orchestra, for brass ensemble, and for woodwind instruments with piano — hoping that something in one or other category
would be found suitable for performance during the period of our visit.
On our arrival we learnt that *all five* works were to be performed later
that week in a public concert by a chamber ensemble with seven soloists
from the orchestra of Moscow Radio; and that the whole programme
was to be simultaneously recorded for commercial issue on disc. The
event was as successful as the composers could possibly have wished;
thanks to extensive rehearsal our music was admirably played to a large,
mainly young, and enthusiastic audience. Only our interpreter was disappointed; he had (we felt) been hoping that our music would prove to
be an avant-garde slap-in-the-face for the Soviet Establishment. (It was
in vain that we tried to explain that in our country the avant-garde *were*
the Establishment.)

There is a price to be paid for everything; and in both Moscow and
Leningrad we had to listen to a stupefying quantity of tapes of music
by Soviet composers. The best (a fraction of the whole) impressed us
greatly, notably a symphony by Karen Khatachurian (nephew of the
famous Aram) and a piano concerto by Boris Tischenko. We met both
these young composers personally, and were agreeably surprised to learn
that the latter was at work on a Russian translation of George Perle's
book on serialism. In both cities the Union had arranged a reception
for us. In Moscow our host — genial enough, though the tinted glasses
which he was obliged to wear to protect weak eyes gave him a suitably
sinister appearance — was the chief secretary, Tikhon Khrennikov.
Khrennikov is widely reviled in the West for the part he played in
engineering the downfall of Shostakovitch at the 1948 Congress. Even
so, it is difficult not to admire the skill with which, like a Marxist Vicar
of Bray, he has managed to retain his hold on power despite every shift
of Party policy. Western critics, understandably eager to discredit
Khrennikov, sometimes make the foolish mistake of denigrating his
capacity as a musician. We were presented with a record of his Piano
Concerto, opus one, from which it was quite clear that as a young man
he was both a talented composer and a very able pianist.

The reception in Leningrad was a disaster. It turned out that we were
expected to give some account of musical conditions in England, past
and present, yet every musical illustration was taken as the signal for
an immediate outbreak of private conversation. We were sustained
throughout the long ordeal by the sight of a row of shapely bottles,
attractively crowned with tinfoil, obviously due to be opened as soon as

11

the fraternal exchange of views had run its alloted course. Alas for our hopes of champagne: the bottles contained nothing more revivifying than sparkling lemonade.

Our next destination was Armenia. Here the principal resident composer was Edward Mirzoyan*, with whom we had already made friends on his visit to London the previous year. The contrast with teetotal Leningrad was almost unbelievable. Brandy flowed like water, even at breakfast-time. And whereas in Leningrad the main ecclesiastical buildings had all been turned into museums designed to pillory the Orthodox Church under the Tsars for its worldliness and wealth, in Armenia churches and cathedrals were in full working order, and moreover officially approved for visiting by state-sponsored delegations such as ours. (The Armenians are very proud that their conversion to Christianity anticipated Rome by some years.)

In Yerevan, the capital, we learnt yet more about the power of the Composers' Union. Their local headquarters, containing administrative offices, recording studio, publishing house and concert hall, is built on one of the best sites in the city; it is flanked by two tiers of luxury flats available for letting only to members of the Union. One of these, naturally, was the home of Mirzoyan, and we were invited there to sample traditional Armenian cooking. While the meal was being prepared we sat on the balcony in the warm autumn sunshine looking towards Mount Ararat — resting place of the Ark, sacred symbol of the Armenian nation and (such are international politics) the property of the Turkish Government. The flat was a house-agent's dream; but considered as a composer's work-place it was less than ideal. Housing shortages are acute in the USSR, and the flat had therefore to provide accommodation not only for Mirzoyan's immediate family but also (if a Gilbertian exaggeration is permissable) for his sisters and his cousins and his aunts.

As a necessity rather than a luxury, therefore, the Soviet Composers' Union has set up throughout Russia a number of retreats where composers can stay for periods of up to two months in order to work on a specific (and approved) project. The Armenian 'Creative house' (this is the official term) occupies a most attractive site at Dilizhan, presented to the Union by the State free of charge. In the grounds are the dozen or so widely separated cottages (or *dachas*) each equipped with grand piano and tape recorder, where visiting composers work and sleep; a central block where meals are taken; and various sporting facilities for

---

* Aram Khatachurian, whom we were to meet later, lived in Moscow. Mirzoyan's best-known composition is the Symphony for timpani and strings.

relaxation. (The cottage assigned to us had recently been occupied by Shostakovitch during the composition of the sunniest of his late quartets, the tenth.) However comfortable the accommodation, the thought of so many composers so industriously at work at such close quarters is, to a Westerner, uncomfortably suggestive of factory farming. And certainly some of the products we sampled had all the blandness of a mass-produced English egg.

From Dilizhan we were driven at terrifying speed by the Union's own Armenian chauffeur, Stepan — a man who used the horn and the accelerator as the chief outlet for his creative personality — to Tbilisi, capital of Georgia and our last stopping point before returning to Moscow. As had been the case with Mirzoyan, we had previously made the acquaintance of Machavariani (the Georgian composer-in-chief) through our own Composers' Guild, and this led to an invitation to lunch at his private *dacha* in the hills above Tbilisi. Here we were entertained with sucking pig, local wine drunk from saucers and — the curse of all Russian social occasions — interminable speeches coupled with toasts 'to friendship' during which all the food got cold. With characteristic Russian kindness, Machavariani's wife presented each of us with a bottle of her home-made sauce whose recipe we had much admired; unfortunately the long return journey across Europe shook it up so violently that (since it was rapidly assuming the appearance of a Molotov cocktail) it had to be discarded in the dustbin for fear of a fatal accident.

To return to the role of the Composers' Union in Soviet musical life: the social benefits of membership are clearly considerable — family accommodation, visits to 'creative houses' and (not hitherto mentioned) sickness benefits. It offers equally important assistance to the composer in his professional life. The Union acts as an agency, putting members in touch with the producers of plays, films and television features. It offers commissions, especially to younger composers who are unable to command them from other sources at the outset of their careers. (If the resulting work proves commercially successful, the commissioning fee is returnable to the Union to help other beginners.) It has its own publishing house and recording studios, it has facilities for copying orchestral parts, and it sponsors concerts, primarily of contemporary music. The Union is enabled to do all these things because of its political and financial muscle. Politically, the Union is a branch of the Government; distinguished composers may be elected to membership of the Supreme Soviet, and one of the deputy Ministers of Culture is normally drawn from the Union's ranks. Its financial strength comes from a central fund, to which every musical event has to contribute a percentage of its takings, irrespective of copyright. (In other words, using the music of the dead does not, as in the West, exempt organisations from their duty to support the living.) Membership is open to all composers and writers of music who have shown both talent and professional commitment for at least two years after graduating. (At the time of our visit enrollment stood at roughly 1,500.)

So much for the advantages of membership: what of the obligations? To adopt the jargon beloved of Marxist spokesmen, a Soviet composer's music must first and foremost be 'part and parcel of the people's life, of the struggle for Communism'. It is to be judged by its 'militant party spirit, Communist ideology, civic ardour and optimism'. Decoded, this means that a Soviet audience should feel uplifted as it leaves the concert hall after a recital of contemporary music, just as a Christian audience feels uplifted after a performance of the *St Matthew Passion*. But whereas a Christian will experience a renewal of his spiritual faith in another world, a Communist will experience a renewal of his belief in a socialist society, already being brought about in this present world by means of unremitting labour and unswerving loyalty to Leninist dogma. In pursuit of this aim, Soviet composers try to write music with an immediate impact, to avoid introspection (except in chamber music, which is recognised as intended for a specialist audience), and to crown large-scale works with triumphantly assertive finales. More specifically, élitism and experiment for its own sake are discouraged; though there is nothing to prevent a composer using aleatoric and other advanced techniques (as Rodion Shchedrin does in his Second and Third Piano Concertos) within an approachable context. Versatility is highly prized; during our visit to Armenia we heard a group of serial piano pieces in the morning and a deafening pop song in the evening by the same composer, Babajanian. Music for young people is also in great demand: Shostakovitch's Second Piano Concerto and his Concertino for two pianos were both written for student performers. (Despite the experimental nature of his music for adults, Maxwell Davies would certainly be *persona grata* in the USSR, on the strength of his music for children.)

On any dispassionate view these demands are surely not unreasonable, though in some respects (such as the inhibition of experiment) perhaps unwise. Palestrina would have found them no more restrictive than the obligation to write the *Missa Papae Marcelli* in conformity with the decrees of the Council of Trent, and Purcell, required to compose odes to celebrate James II's accession and subsequent deposition with equal enthusiasm, would have had no difficulty in coping with the rise and fall of Stalin's 'cult of personality'. Only for the past 150 years has it been considered outrageous for the payer of the piper to insist on his right to call the tune.

The fundamental objection to the Soviet system is that it is a monopoly — buttressed by the threat of withdrawal of Union membership, with all its privileges. If for any reason a composer cannot bring himself to work within the conditions prescribed by the State, there is no other employer to whom he may turn. The alternatives are conformity or silence. If he persistently disregards the requirements of his only customer he will find himself labelled a 'bourgeois formalist' (that handy catch-all phrase), and his music will be neither published or performed until some cataclysmic event like the death of Stalin alters the political climate.

We like to congratulate ourselves that in our own country there are no such pressures. But there is more than one way of killing cats and composers. Here, every aspect of the music industry is governed almost entirely by commercial considerations. In recent years we have seen long-established publishing and recording companies absorbed by larger concerns anxious to 'diversify'; meanwhile, escalating production costs have compelled firms to promote only composers with a profit-making potential. The doctrines of business management schools have been swallowed wholesale, with the scarcely credible result that printed music is liable to be destroyed and recordings deleted almost without notice — on the grounds that by occupying desirable shelf-space they are not just failing to make money, they are actually losing it.

In a similar way, most of our performing institutions have as little as possible to do with the living British composer on the pretext — and here the musical public must be held largely responsible — that he is box-office poison. The programmes given at the Royal Festival Hall by the principal London orchestras speak for themselves. During the 1978–79 season 463 works were performed and of these precisely 11 were by the players' fellow-countrymen. The figures for the previous year were 461 and 12 respectively. Chamber orchestras did better — but not much. Sixteen works by living British composers out of a total of 207 were performed during the 1978–79 season, and the year before, nineteen out of 212. (In both cases, be it noted, the figures show an appalling situation deteriorating still further.)* A contributory cause is the readiness of London orchestral managements to engage foreign conductors without first stipulating that they must actively promote the British instrumental repertory. There seems no good reason for exempting them from an

---

* This statistical analysis was prepared for the Composers' Guild by Bernard Barrell.

obligation which in the 19th century was more than conscientiously discharged by men of the calibre of Hallé, Richter and Richard Wagner.

One organisation alone can to a limited extent afford to disregard commercial considerations — the BBC; and without it the position of the living composer would indeed be desperate. Contemporary music in a wide range of styles is generously represented on Radio 3; that this should be so is in large measure due to producers like Hans Keller, who have insisted on the inclusion of music which they themselves disliked but nevertheless believed to be significant. A score submitted to the BBC for possible performance will always receive careful consideration, regardless of whether the composer's name is known or unknown; in the latter case a panel of musicians from outside the Corporation will usually be asked to reach a verdict. Unfortunately there is only one BBC, so that a monopoly situation obtains here precisely as it does in Russia. (Wales and Scotland have a separate broadcasting identity, but concern themselves almost exclusively with composers who have local affiliations.) What is more, two men — the Controller of the Music Division, which prepares the programmes, and the Controller of Radio 3, which presents them — have dictatorial powers such as a Soviet Commissar might envy. For a period of 13 years the former kept all the BBC's public concerts under his sole control, designing the programmes in accordance with his own personal likes and dislikes. It was little consolation for a whole generation of composers who found themselves excluded from the Proms to be told that this suppression had nothing to do with politics. In 1975 the latter, a Viennese by birth, happened to pay a visit to Covent Garden to hear *Rosenkavalier*. Overcome with nostalgia, he cancelled all the programmes scheduled for broadcasting the following Saturday at four days' notice, so that the Strauss opera could be relayed (in German) to the British public. There was no appeal against this decision, although this meant cancelling the advertised première of a new opera by a living British composer. (It was the same Controller who, at similar short notice, cancelled another evening's programmes with another British première so that listeners could enjoy the amazing sensation of hearing Mozart's *Marriage of Figaro* performed in the presence of M. Pompidou.)

It may be objected that British musical organisations can, if they wish, free themselves from commercial as well as political pressures by applying for one of the subsidies distributed through the Arts Council. Unfortunately these subsidies are by European standards wholly inadequate; only about a quarter of the income of a London orchestra comes from this source, whereas roughly half is earned by recording sessions. One astonishing feature of these subsidies is that they are awarded unconditionally; performers incur no obligation whatever to play any British music in return for handouts of British money. The awards are made by a board of Government appointees, drawn mainly from the world of the arts; the board is assisted by panels of experts whose advice, however, *they are not obliged to take.* (Members of these panels are initially appointed — not elected — for a period of three years. It is difficult for them to institute reforms, since it takes the best part of three years to learn how the system works.) Implementation of decisions is entrusted to a staff of permanent officers, whose enthusiasm or otherwise for the board's proposals obviously make a considerable difference to their ultimate success. (A Government minister is similarly dependent on the whole-hearted co-operation of his permanent civil servants.)

Two examples of the system in action must suffice. Some years ago the advisory panel was so incensed by the failure of British orchestras to play British music, in spite of a whole series of incentive schemes, that it demanded a reversal of the ruling that subsidies should be given without strings. So intense was the pressure on the Arts Council that the chairman was forced to yield to the extent of summoning the orchestral managements and informing them that unless they were prepared to mend their ways voluntarily, coercion would have to be applied. Within two years the advocates of reform had left the panel after completing their period of office; their protest sank without trace, and London orchestral life resumed the even tenor of its ways. (It is worth adding that the recipient of the board's biggest subsidy — the Royal Opera House, Covent Garden — is not subject to the scrutiny of any advisory panel at all.)

The other incident concerned gramophone records. A sum of money was already at the disposal of the British Council for subsidising the recording of music by British composers; and it was proposed that a similar sum should be allocated by the Arts Council for the same purpose. In order to prevent yet another monopoly situation arising, a panel member suggested that there should be two separate schemes run by two separate committees; this would give a second chance to any composer whose recording project was turned down by the British Council (a not infrequent occurrence). This ran into objections from the permanent officials, on the score of duplication of effort (and a corresponding increase in administrative costs). A compromise was eventually reached: there should be one scheme and one committee, but the Arts Council would submit its own recommendations to the British Council along with its cheque. The result was as might have been foreseen: the cheque was accepted, and the recommendation (for a pioneer recording of music by Havergal Brian and Cyril Scott) rejected.

The only body* that exists to safeguard composers' rights is the Composers Guild of Great Britain; unlike the Musicians' Union (which protects performers) it has no leverage to apply in support of its members' interests, since any threat to withdraw their labour would be counterproductive. Apart from such grants as it can obtain from sponsors, the Guild's source of finance is the subscriptions of its membership, scarcely an affluent body. In all these circumstances it was surely a remarkable achievement to establish a British Music Information Centre, with a full-time librarian and its own journal, *The Composer*. (The BMIC is now run as an independent trust.) The Guild, through its general secretary, is always available to help members with advice on contracts, or support in obtaining redress for professional grievances. A few years ago it succeeded in frustrating an ingenious plan for enabling film companies to retain half the royalties due to a composer for a commissioned score by the delightfully simple method of nominating themselves the publishers. (The beauty of the plan was that it didn't involve the expense of actually printing the music.) For many years the Guild has also successfully participated in exchange schemes with other countries; and the fact that composers visiting England have for financial reasons been entertained mainly in private houses has had the beneficial reciprocal effects described earlier in this chapter. Even so, many such exchange proposals have had to be turned down for lack of funds; and the continued existence of the BMIC journal and even of the Guild itself is currently threatened by inflation.

The boasted independence of the British composer, as opposed to his Soviet counterpart, can be therefore seen to be largely illusory. He too works under a monopoly system, and he too is under pressure (in his case, commercial) to conform. We are entitled to take some comfort from the assurance that British, unlike Russian, musicians are not subject to thought control; but we delude ourselves if we suppose that the motive is halfway creditable. The anxiety of the Soviet authorities to exercise the strictest supervision over composers results from the belief that the emotions aroused by music have the power to influence, for good or ill, the life and character of every individual citizen. (That was also the reason for the primacy of music in the educational system of ancient Athens, and for the influence upon society ascribed to melody by Plato in his *Republic*.) If the freedom permitted to composers in this country were really due to toleration, it would indeed be a cause of rejoicing. In fact, however, it is just a by-product of philistine indifference.

---

* A splinter group called the Association of Professional Musicians has recently been formed.

3. David and Goliath I

The visit of John Gardner and myself to Tbilisi described in the previous chapter had, four years later, a curious sequel. Opening the latest Stravinsky-Craft compilation *Dialogues and a Diary*, I was astounded to read that Stravinsky had been mightily impressed by some tapes of Georgian *Krimanchuli* singing 'recorded by Noah Greenberg in mountain villages near Tiflis (Tbilisi)'. This alleged discovery by Greenberg of 'an active performing tradition of music ranging from 10th-century conductus and organum to High Renaissance' was, Stravinsky claimed, a major find. He placed his own anti-Soviet gloss on this episode: 'needless to say, this exhumed treasure, being both foreign and religious in origin and therefore embarrassing to progressive historicism, and polyphonic and therefore subversive, is unwelcome in the Soviet Union and unlikely to be preserved. No doubt it will be ploughed in again for good, and replaced by Moscow-manufactured party-slogan songs ...'

A natural eagerness to put the record straight was much enhanced by my detestation of demonstrably false Cold War propaganda. How to go about it, however, was far from obvious. I did not wish to impute deliberate fabrication where there might have been only innocent misunderstanding; moreover, one of the participants was dead and the other among the few indisputably great composers of our century. In the end I decided to present the matter as one of musico-ethnological interest, and wrote to the editor of the journal *Composer* as follows:

> The discovery which Noah Greenberg *personally* made in Tiflis was not of an ancient tradition of polyphonic singing, but of two more recent and much less interesting curiosities — to be precise, John Gardner and myself, then in Georgia as delegates of the Composers' Guild to the USSR. Greenberg had with him a party of singers and instrumentalists and was giving a series of three concerts in Tiflis, one entire programme of which was devoted to English music of the Elizabethan period. (I am able to be precise because I kept a diary of our trip, which saves me from having to rely on a capricious memory.) Hearing that we had been invited to the Conservatoire to listen to a programme of Georgian folkmusic, Greenberg asked to be allowed to 'tag along'. It was at this session that Greenberg first heard — as we did — recordings of traditional Georgian polyphonic singing, including that extraordinary virile yodelling which Stravinsky terms *Krimanchuli* (in an article on my return I compared its sound to the war-cries of Achilles in the second act of Tippett's *King Priam*.) The Director of the Conservatoire proved that

this was still a living tradition in Georgia, not only by singing himself as points which required illustration arose in the course of discussion, but also by calling in from the corridor a passing group of students to give an extempore performance of a three-part song which we had previously heard in a recorded version. We listened to sacred as well as secular music, choral as well as instrumental, and on leaving we were each presented with a selection of tapes and published texts to take back home to our respective countries.

This clearly makes nonsense of the claim (not necessarily advanced by Greenberg himself) that it was Greenberg who discovered this treasure trove in 'mountain villages near Tiflis'. It is just possible that he made some journeys into the surrounding country outside Tiflis *after* making the acquaintance of this music in our company, but I regard this as highly unlikely in view of his tight concert schedule. But even if he did so, he cannot have discovered and subsequently transmitted to Stravinsky anything that the three of us had not already heard; for Stravinsky's remarks are an exact description of the music which had been played on tape and performed for us that morning by the Director of the Conservatoire.

It makes even more nonsense of the anti-Soviet inferences drawn from the episode by Stravinsky. To say that 'this exhumed treasure is ... unwelcome and unlikely to be preserved' is the precise opposite of the case, since it is demonstrably not only being preserved but actively cultivated. Incidentally, these inferences would have been false even if Stravinsky's account of the 'discovery' had been correct; for Greenberg could never have gone into mountain villages near Tiflis and made recordings without the active encouragement and co-operation of the authorities. Moreover, as anyone at all familiar with the USSR knows, it is Party policy to stimulate, rather than 'plough under', manifestations of local culture (this helps to give an illusion of autonomy while the real power is concentrated at the centre); and it was no surprise to find, when later the same day we visited the leading Georgian composer Machavariani at his *dacha* outside Tiflis, that he was even then incorporating passages of traditional Georgian religious music ('embarrassing to progressive historicism') into his latest composition.

It is entirely natural for Stravinsky, a White Russian, to have a built-in prejudice against Soviet Communism; but it is a pity he has given way to it in his latest book since (owing to his unique position in the world of music) any statement he makes is liable to be accepted as authoritative. After all, there are plenty of real grounds for complaint in Soviet musical theory and practice without inventing non existent ones.

How this article came to Stravinsky's attention in Hollywood, California, I do not know; but he clearly thought that a magisterial rebuke was called for. His reply began with an objection to my use of the word ethnomusicology, and continued (by way of a pun on the names of Greenberg and Monteverdi) with the reassertion that 'obviously Mr Greenberg's discovery was purely his own':

What Mr Greenberg *did* say, to the best of my recollection, was that the music performed by his New York group, and the resemblances noted in it to the music of the local tradition, had excited the interest of Georgian musicians. Then, as I understood it, after his concerts Mr Greenberg and two or three members of his ensemble were taken to villages near Tiflis, where they performed for the villagers and the villagers for them.

But my recollection is rickety, and it is several years since Mr Greenberg played his tapes for me. In fact I would be inclined to believe in Mr Bush's doubts and call the story a daydream, except for one circumstance: I am positive that my wife and Mr Greenberg compared notes about two villages near Tiflis in which she had lived and which Mr Greenberg most certainly had visited.

The remainder of the letter was devoted to a defence of Stravinsky's anti-Soviet attitude. It referred to the 'USSR's policy of *suppressing* manifestations of religious culture (notoriously of late in the case of the Jews)' and the 'policy of cultural containment', reports of which had recently been brought back from Tiflis by George Balanchine after a visit to his brother, Balanchivadze, the Georgian composer. Stravinsky ended his letter (dated 1st April 1969):

> May I add that not long before his death, Mr Greenberg gave me some additional tapes of the music, and that my pleasure was as great at the later date as at the time of the first experience.

The way was now open to make clear that there were only two possible explanations for Stravinsky's original misstatement: either he had completely misunderstood Greenberg or the latter had issued what the Companies' Act would describe as a false prospectus. To express this in unmistakeable terms and yet at the same time with the courtesy due to a man 'never to be named without reverence of musicians' remained an exceedingly difficult task, and I still have no idea whether or not I succeeded:

> The most recent standard English dictionary defines the word discover: 'to find out *for the first time*' (my italics). In 'Dialogues and a Diary' Stravinsky expressly uses the words *discovery* and a *major find* of the late Noah Greenberg's activities in Tiflis. The facts are as stated in my original article. Stravinsky cannot refute them; we were there, he was not. Greenberg became acquainted *for the first time* with *Krimanchuli* and the rest during his visit to the Tiflis Conservatoire; the invitation to the Conservatoire he owed to John Gardner and myself, the information he acquired there he owed to the Director. Stravinsky cannot impugn my memory of these events; they were noted in my journal the day they occurred. Greenberg may have visited Georgian villages subsequently — indeed, I expressly allowed for that

possibility in my original article — but he could not have done this without the express permission, or rather the active co-operation, of the Georgian authorities. In a word, Greenberg did not track down a hidden treasure; he was simply invited, as we were, to admire an openly-displayed national possession. In *Dialogues and a Diary*, Stravinsky states that the tapes played to him were recorded by Greenberg himself in the mountain villages which he visited near Tiflis. If he will pardon the Runyon-ism, I will take a piece of six to five that they were copies of tapes which were given to the three of us by the Director of the Conservatoire. If Stravinsky will send a transcript of the ones presented to him by Greenberg which are presumably in his possession, it should be possible to verify this. Should my statement prove incorrect, I undertake to ask the editor of *Composer* to publish a retraction.

How is one to account for the discrepancy between Greenberg's actual activities and the account of them given by Stravinsky in *Dialogues and a Diary?* Like the headstrong king bullying Teiresias in his own *Oedipus Rex*, Stravinsky compels me to be more explicit than I hoped would be necessary. I expressly used the phrase to which he takes exception 'not necessarily advanced by Greenberg himself' to allow for the possibility of a misunderstanding by Stravinsky rather than a misstatement by Greenberg. The only alternative is, simply, that Greenberg was not telling the truth. This does not necessarily imply that there was any *deliberate* falsification; in retelling from memory an episode in which one has participated, it frequently happens that one imperceptibly alters the sequence of events until one appears as enacting the role one *wishes* one had played, rather than the role one actually did play. (By the time he had finished describing the fight on Gadshill, Falstaff was undoubtedly perfectly convinced that he had single-handed taken on eleven men in buckram).

The minatory tone of Stravinsky's reply and his deliberate choice of words like *misconstruction, wilfully naive, nicely precise, casual* in order to suggest to the reader that I am not to be trusted, makes me wonder whether Stravinsky suspects me of being 'soft on Communism'. I am indeed soft on the *ideal* which inspired Communism, but for that very reason implacably opposed to a régime which has betrayed that ideal. I would be the first to agree with Stravinsky that the Soviet Government is atheistic and anti-semitic. If, however, we accuse them of crimes which they have not committed, we merely destroy our own credibility. It is abundantly plain that they *do* (whatever the motive) encourage manifestations of local culture, even at the price of exempting a particular area from religious persecution. For proof of this one has only to contrast the different treatment accorded to cathedrals in Leningrad (which are open to the public as anti-God museums) and the one at Etchmiadzin (which is in full use as the headquarters of the Armenian Church). Prejudice is fine (as Stravinsky surmises, I have plenty of my own) but as a weapon it is useless; it recoils too often upon the user.

Stravinsky did not take up the challenge. Instead, his original letter was subsequently republished in a final collection of his writings without

explanation or retraction. That any reply to Stravinsky was possible —
or had actually been made — was nowhere mentioned. This was perhaps
to be expected. Less readily explicable was the fact that a copy only of
Stravinsky's letter was sent to *Composer*, and a request for a signed
original was refused (on what purported to be Stravinsky's own instructions) by his English representative. I can only deduce that this was in
aid of a future Stravinsky archive; but it leads me to wonder whether
to abstract a composer's writings before his death in aid of an archive
differs morally from abstracting his kidneys in aid of a transplant
operation. (The risks, like the benefits, are admittedly not comparable.)
Such a train of thought inevitably leads one to wonder exactly how far
Stravinsky himself was aware of, or gave his approval to, such a proceeding. Perhaps the composition referred to in my second statement
should not have been the master's *Oedipus Rex* but *Petrouchka*.

4. A morning with Rostropovitch

That a performer of genius should wish to lay aside his instrument and take up conducting comes as a surprise, especially when one considers that conductors as a race — with a few notable exceptions — are not greatly admired by their fellow professionals. (Saint-Saëns once told Beecham, who had just conducted a concert of his music: 'My dear young friend, I have lived a long while, and I have known all the *chefs d'orchestre*. There are two kinds: one who takes the music too fast, and the other too slow. There is no third.') But conducting is no mere interlude in Rostropovitch's career as a master cellist: it is the fulfilment of a life's ambition. Everything else that he has done is to be regarded as leading up to it.

Landmarks in his career have been his début as a concert conductor in the city of Gorki in 1961, and as an opera conductor at the Bolshoi Theatre in 1968 (directing Tschaikowsky's *Eugene Onegin*). He never took a formal course of lessons in conducting but, as he himself explains, all the conductors for whom he has ever played have in a sense acted as his teachers. He admires individuality in an interpreter, and for that reason prefers yesterday's conductors to today's, who turn out polished performances barely distinguishable one from another (like so many Hilton Hotels of music). When preparing for his British début four years ago he studied recordings of the opening item (Rossini's overture *The Silken Ladder*) made by Beecham and Toscanini — and discovered that the Italian's performance was nearly twice as fast as the Englishman's. (His own interpretation, he suggested, was somewhere in-between, but with a slight inclination towards Beecham.) Like Chekhov's character Trofimov, Rostropovitch can claim to be the eternal student, always willing (and able) to learn from the example of others. Far from thinking that he, as a Russian, knew everything there was to be known about Tschaikowsky, Rostropovitch made a special study of the interpretation of the German Furtwängler, which proved to be profoundly illuminating. (Such open-mindedness is in marked contrast to the attitude of English musicians when Casals first played the Elgar Cello Concerto over here: Casals' interpretation was un-English, and therefore inadmissable.)

Rostropovitch spoke with great affection and respect of another cellist turned conductor — John Barbirolli, whom he first met in person when they served together on the jury of the Pablo Casals competition in Paris in 1957. To have been a string player (and particularly a great one) is a tremendous advantage to a conductor; he commands the immediate respect of his orchestra (who know that everything they can do he can do better) and can personally supervise the doings of the string section — 'the life-blood of the orchestra'. Like Barbirolli, Rostropovitch requires his string players to use his own bowings, and has advised Prokofiev and other composers on the most suitable string phrasings to be marked in their scores — a similar service to that provided by Joachim for Brahms. But Rostropovitch does not believe that there is only one correct way of performing a work. He recalls, wryly, that Shostakovitch took a tape of the première of the First Cello Concerto, and (because he enjoyed the performance) based all the metronome markings in the printed score on those particular tempi. Years later, having really penetrated to the heart of the work through constant study and performance, Rostropovitch came to the conclusion that his original interpretation was too slow; yet if today he performs it at a quicker speed, he runs the ironical risk of being criticised for disregarding the composer's published instructions.

Shostakovitch was Rostropovitch's teacher for composition at the Moscow Conservatory. In 1949 came his first disillusionment with the régime: Shostakovitch, disgraced the previous year at the Composers' Union Congress presided over by the iniquitous Zhdanov, was actually dismissed from his teaching post, and Rostropovitch felt 'compelled by conscience' to leave the Conservatory. (Fortunately he had already graduated as a cellist, but as a composer he remains academically unqualified — for what that is worth — to this day.) Their relationship can best be described in the words of Webern's birthday tribute to Schoenberg: 'friend and pupil: one was always the same as the other'. Their last meeting, in May 1974, was another unforgettable, tragic event. Rostropovitch, having decided that it was impossible for him and his wife to continue working in Russia, went to break the news to Skostakovitch, who was already suffering from the disease which was to kill him. Rostropovitch could find no words with which to soften the blow, and at last, speechless, pulled out of his pocket the exit permit signed by Brezhnev.

As a parting promise, Rostropovitch undertook to record Shostakovitch's major works at the earliest opportunity: all the symphonies ('but don't do the first three' interrupted Shostakovitch) and the piece dearest to the composer's heart, *Katerina Ismailova*, in the original version and under its proper title, *Lady Macbeth of Mtensk Province.*

Lady Macbeth was the cause of Shostakovitch's first clash with the

Soviet authorities when, in 1936, the work was banned on Stalin's personal instructions two years after its triumphantly acclaimed first production. It is not easy to disentangle the real reasons for Stalin's disapproval from the standard clichés of Soviet criticism ('bourgeois formalism' and the like). It was evidently found to be too dissonant, too experimental and too explicitly erotic; also it satirised the Tsarist regime (including its secret police) at a time when, for patriotic reasons, this was in process of rehabilitation. Much the same, however, can be said of that masterpiece of Soviet cinema, the Gorki trilogy. But there is one fundamental difference between the two works: Shostakovitch's opera ends in unrelieved blackness, as the prisoners set off to their Siberian exile sustained by not the slightest glimmer of hope. In complete contrast, the three chapters of Gorki's autobiography all end with the screen a blaze of sunlight, and the youthful characters look forward with unshakeable optimism to the dawn of a glorious Soviet future.

Over 30 years after the banning of his opera, Shostakovitch was offered the chance of a new production on condition that he revised it. He jumped at the opportunity, though he would have much preferred to leave the work unaltered. Even after most of the original asperities had been smoothed out ('to make it easier on the ears') the opera was not allocated a performance at the Bolshoi, but assigned to the smaller Stanislavsky, a theatre with a vastly inferior orchestra. This was more than Rostropovitch could stand. Although he had never yet appeared as a rank-and-file member of an orchestra — as a potential international soloist he had been excused all orchestral rehearsals at the Conservatory — Rostropovitch collected a dozen or so of his string-playing friends and they all sat in the pit to augment the Stanislavsky band for the first performance.

Rostropovitch contrasts this revision under duress with the corrected versions of his own work made by Prokofiev. These were invariably the result of inner conviction. In 1947, Prokofiev heard Rostropovitch play his Cello Concerto in E minor, Op. 58, accompanied by a fellow student playing from the piano reduction. This made the composer realise that he hadn't made the best use of his musical material, and decided him to subject it to a complete reworking. Consequently there is now a second Prokofiev Cello Concerto (actually entitled Sinfonia Concertante, Op. 125) which, though it uses the same themes as the first, is a completely independant composition. And it is this second version which bears the composer's final seal of approval. Prokofiev later began work on another contribution to the cello repertory, the Concertino in G minor, Op. 132; after the composer's death the almost-completed sketches were finished and orchestrated by Rostropovitch in collaboration with Kabalevsky.

I ventured to suggest that although Prokofiev was (for me) one of the greatest of 20th-century composers, yet by all accounts he was a difficult person to get on with. 'Not difficult; just truthful.' After the disastrous première of the (original) Cello Concerto in 1938, Prokofiev went backstage to the green-room, but remained silent. Eventually the conductor pressed him to deliver his verdict. Prokofiev looked him straight in the eye and replied: 'It couldn't have gone worse.'

We hear little or nothing in England about the musical heirs of Shostakovitch and Prokofiev, although (according to Rostropovitch) there is any amount of talent in the USSR. But its development continues to be hampered by the repressive behaviour of the authorities. Among the most promising of the younger composers are Piart (Lithuania),* Silvestrov (Kiev) and Sidelnikov (Moscow). When I told Rostropovitch that in response to a request for recordings of recent Soviet music the Composers' Union had sent me a tape of a work by Arvo Pärt, he commented drily: 'Then it won't be one of his best pieces.' He also spoke enthusiastically of Boris Chaikowsky and of Boris Tischenko, a Shostakovitch pupil from Leningrad. He acknowledged that Rodion Shchedrin was an outstandingly gifted composer, but feared that his official position (as one of the seven Secretaries of the Composers' Union) might tempt him into compromise.

Life for any adventurous young composer in the USSR is undoubtedly difficult. Even commissioned works may never achieve performance, or if performed once with triumphant success — as was the case with the *Lermontov* symphony for voice and chamber orchestra by Nicolai Sidelnikov — are never heard of again. Provincial concerts are also carefully monitored. When a symphony by Alfred Schnittke was announced for performance in Gorki under the direction of Rozhdestvensky, a large audience of musicians travelled from Moscow to hear it, although Gorki is a day's journey from the capital. The composer was immediately required to give an account of himself: 'What do you mean by sloping off to Gorki and getting up to your formalist tricks there?'

By a coincidence, on the day before our conversation the London *Evening Standard* had carried an article complaining that all but a favoured inner circle of British composers had been excluded from the Proms during the dictatorial régime of William Glock (thirteen years) and Robert Ponsonby (three years). Rostropovitch agreed that as far as orchestral concerts were concerned, life was every bit as difficult for a British composer who was *non persona grata* with the management as it was for a

* Composer of a *Cantus* in memory of Benjamin Britten.

27

Russian one. But at least our recital halls are open to all, whereas in the USSR even the solo concert is subject to strict supervision and censorship. Rostropovitch cited as an example a song recital given by himself and his wife, the soprano Galina Vishnevskya: a song-cycle by Boris Chaikowsky was officially deleted from the published programme because the Ministry of Culture objected to the texts by the poet Brodsky. Only during the Kruschev era had any measure of artistic freedom been permitted, and Rostropovitch looked back on those as 'the good days'.

But the Soviet government's greatest crime remains its treatment of Shostakovitch. Rostropovitch contrasted the master in his early years — bursting with ideas, energetic, ebullient, tirelessly interested in innovation, writing music whose youthful genius exploded out of every bar — with the withdrawn, haunted figure whose spirit had been crushed by a series of public humiliations until by the end he had become, literally, a broken man. What works might he not have written in his maturity if his creative fire had not been systematically smothered by the authorities? It is difficult to criticise such a view from the side-lines; none the less, I feel it to be mistaken in the light of the extraordinary achievements of Shostakovitch's final period — the last three symphonies and the last group of string quartets, works rarely equalled and never surpassed throughout the whole of musical history. In them Shostakovitch, like Beethoven, attains that purification of style and profundity of thought which come even to the greatest of composers only after experiencing the depths of human unhappiness. But Rostropovitch was not to be persuaded: 'Beethoven's deafness was incurable; Shostakovitch's suffering was man-made, and could have been prevented.'

What then of Russia's greatest literary survivor, his friend Solzhenitsyn? 'I would like you to tell your readers: he is a giant among men'. For four years Rostropovitch provided a home for the disgraced writer, during which time he worked every day from six in the morning until ten at night. His average expenditure on himself was about 20 pence a day — for a diet of spaghetti, cabbage and soup. If there is a single word that for Rostropovitch sums up the character of Solzhenitsyn it is: truth. Perhaps the two men were attracted to each other because they were opposites. Rostropovitch, by nature full of the joy of life, wants to communicate love and happiness to others through the medium of his music; Solzhenitsyn has that darker, introverted character to be found in many other great Russian writers, such as Dostoievsky. Also 'Solzhenitsyn carries the whole world in his head, whereas I am thinking only about a handful of notes in a musical score.' But the picture of Solzhenitsyn as a morose hermit barricaded behind a barbed-wire fence in Vermont is utterly false. To his friends he is as readily accessible as ever; and if he keeps his family under close protection he has very good reasons for doing so. (Trotsky did not succeed in avoiding vengeance simply by settling in Mexico.)

Finally, we spoke of Rostropovitch's future plans. It is characteristic of his humanity and generosity that his ambition is to repay the debt incurred to the older musicians who launched him on his musical career, by helping the younger musicians who will one day succeed him. One idea is to celebrate the centenary of *Eugene Onegin* at the Aldeburgh Festival by performing it with a cast of talented singers all with their names still to make — a most appropriate celebration, since Tschai- kowsky's opera was originally given by students of the Moscow Conservatory.* He also hopes to perform and, opportunity permitting, record music by British composers. He sees himself as helping to build on the foundations laid by his friend Benjamin Britten, and playing a subsidiary role in support of those who, like Peter Pears, knew Britten best. How fortunate that when the Soviet authorities 'Like the base Indian, threw a pearl away Richer than all his tribe', we in England were given an opportunity to pick it up.

* This Aldeburgh production subsequently took place.

5. A clash of personalities

In her book *An unfinished woman*, Lillian Hellman describes the difficulty she found in assessing the accounts of Soviet Russia given her by American journalists and diplomats on the occasion of her first visit to that country: '... one couldn't pick the true charges from the wild hatred ... some of what they said in those days most certainly turned out to be the truth, but it is hard to understand fact from invention when it is mixed with blind bitterness about a place and people.' This could not be bettered as a diagnosis of what is wrong with a book purporting to emanate from the USSR itself — *Testimony*, 'the memoirs of Shostakovitch as related to and edited by Solomon Volkov'.

Volkov published the book after Shostakovitch's death (ostensibly in accordance with the composer's own instructions) and after his own emigration to America. Predictably, anti-Soviet hardliners have accepted it as gospel, so that it has proved to be Volkov's passport to academic respectability. Equally predictably it has been dismissed in Russia as a forgery. Which view is correct?

Whatever one's standpoint, it has to be conceded from the start that the portrait of Shostakovitch presented in the book is necessarily incomplete. Volkov never knew the composer as a young man — an innovator in music, a Marxist in politics, and in private life a football fanatic. The Shostakovitch who once declared that he liked people to laugh at his music is wholly missing from Volkov's book; all we get is the sick, disappointed, introverted old man, pre-occupied with 'the bitter experience of my grey and miserable life'. We hear nothing of the joys of creation, of the joys of being heard and understood by a world-wide audience. Of family life, of friends there is no word; no word of colleagues he is known to have admired, like Benjamin Britten. Instead 'there were no particularly happy moments in my life, no great joys. It was grey and dull, and it makes me sad to think about it'.

It is generally agreed that Shostakovitch gave Volkov some half-a-dozen interviews when the latter was working for the magazine *Soviet Music*, and initialled each one as a guarantee of authenticity after they had been written up. Unfortunately, there was nothing to prevent the typescript being tampered with at a later stage, and Maxim Shostakovitch, who told reporters after his defection to the West that he regarded Volkov's portrait of his father as a fabrication, believes this to have been the case. 'Can you imagine that such critical statements as were later published in the book could ever have been made for a Soviet magazine? Volkov probably slotted numerous pages between the unnumbered pages of the interview. It's easily done.' Maxim also challenges the authenticity of the musical opinions ascribed to his father, though it is difficult to see what incentive Volkov could have had for falsifying these. Certainly they are uniformly gloomy; the only musician to be treated with the slightest affection and respect is Shostakovitch's teacher Glazunov, and even he is remembered chiefly for his addiction to alcohol. The most startling discrepancy involves Prokofiev, who emerges from *Testimony* as a mean man and a meaner composer, whereas Maxim recalls 'how highly and favourably' his father spoke of both him and Stravinsky.

In 1934, Prokofiev returned to Soviet Russia after a self-imposed exile of 15 years. It is instructive to compare the reasons given to Serge Moreux by Prokofiev himself with the account of the same episode related (supposedly) by Shostakovitch. Here is Prokofiev: 'Foreign air does not suit my inspiration, because I'm Russian, and that is to say the least suited of men to be an exile, to remain in a psychological climate that isn't of my race ... I've got to go back. I've got to live myself back into the atmosphere of my native soil. I've got to see real winter again, and spring that bursts into being from one moment to the next. I've got to hear the Russian language echoing in my ears, I've got to talk to people who are my own flesh and blood, so that they can give me back something I lack here — their songs — my songs. Here I'm getting enervated. I risk dying of academicism. Yes, my friends! I'm going back.'

Testimony suggests a motive of a very different kind: 'Prokofiev was an inveterate gambler, and, in the long run, he always won. Prokofiev thought that he had calculated perfectly and that he would be a winner this time too. For some 15 years Prokofiev sat between two stools — in the West he was considered a Soviet and in Russia they welcomed him as a Western guest.

'But then the situation changed and the bureaucrats in charge of cultural affairs started squinting at Prokofiev, thinking Who is this Parisian fellow? And Prokofiev considered that it would be more profitable for him to move to the USSR. Such a step would only raise his stock in the West, because things Soviet were becoming fashionable just then, they would stop considering him a foreigner in the USSR, and therefore he would win all round.

'By the way, the final impetus came from his card-playing. Prokofiev was deeply in debt abroad and he had to straighten out his financial affairs quickly, which he hoped to do in the USSR.

'And this was where Prokofiev landed like a chicken in the soup'.

It would be comforting to attribute the malice pervading these paragraphs entirely to Volkov; but it is hard to resist the suspicion that in his heart of hearts Shostakovitch was not best pleased at the sudden appearance of a rival of his own stature in a previously empty field — nor at the rapturous homecoming accorded, appropriately enough, to the composer of *The Prodigal Son*. If Volkov is to be trusted, their dislike was mutual. 'I don't think he ever treated me seriously as a composer' Shostakovitch is reported to have complained, adding that the unpublished correspondence with Miaskovsky contains 'quite a few disparaging remarks about me'. There is nothing inherently improbable in a clash between two such strong personalities. What *is* scarcely credible is the allegation that Shostakovitch was unable to appreciate Prokofiev's skill as an orchestrator. Their approach to the medium was of course entirely different. Shostakovitch (like Beethoven) treated the orchestra as a vehicle for ideas, Prokofiev (like Mozart) for its own sake. Only in their economy of effort did the two composers resemble each other; their scores seldom look good — they simply *sound* good. Even so this does not begin to explain the assertion in *Testimony* that because Prokofiev presumed to differ from his teacher Rimsky-Korsakov 'he never did learn to orchestrate properly'. It is also implied that because Prokofiev employed an amanuensis to prepare his full scores (as did Vaughan Williams), he delegated the actual task of instrumentation to others. Other dunces are stood in the corner alongside Prokofiev: Scriabin 'knew as much about orchestration as a pig about oranges', and Mussourgsky orchestrated the forest scene in *Boris Godunov* 'falteringly and badly, like a student afraid of failing an exam'. Fortunately, Shostakovitch – Volkov was at hand (like the psychoanalyst in Tippett's *The Knot garden*) to put them all to rights. In 1940 *Boris* was rescored, and as for Prokofiev 'I made corrections when I performed his First Piano Concerto *at a very young age*' (my italics).

* * *

Prokofiev himself, in a most perceptive analysis, has identified five elements in his own style: classicism, lyricism, an innovatory approach to harmony, a love of motor rhythms, and wit (this last ranging all the way from simple good humour to satire and burlesque). All five are present in the best of the music written before leaving Russia, for Prokofiev found his own distinctive tone of voice at a very early age: the first two Piano Concertos, the First ('Classical') Symphony, the Second Piano Sonata and (especially notable for its lyricism) the First Violin Concerto.

During the rest of his life no major stylistic changes occurred, only a periodic shift of emphasis. (This suggests that one of the rare compliments paid to Prokofiev in *Testimony* — 'a new period seemed to begin in his work just before his death, he seemed to be feeling along new paths' — was misconceived.) It is true that while he was resident in the West the more modernistic aspects of his music came to the fore in, for example, the last of his piano concertos. But emphasis is still laid on structural logic and economy of means (the twin hallmarks of classicism), and in such scores as the Third Piano Concerto and the ballet *The Prodigal Son* a near-perfect balance between the five stylistic elements is maintained. Hilarity naturally predominates in *The Love for Three Oranges*, the only full-length comic opera written in our century which can make everyone laugh. Everyone, that is, except Shostakovich–Volkov: 'I just find it boring: I'm constantly aware of the composer's attempts at being funny and it's not funny at all.' After comparing the opera unfavourably with his own comedy *The Nose*, he concludes 'It's rather hard to be witty in music — it's too easy to end up with something like *Three Oranges*'. It *is* true that Prokofiev's music is not self-sufficient. For full enjoyment the delightfully absurd fairy-tale has to be brought to life on stage, complete with the confrontation between good wizard (hopelessly incompetent) and wicked witch, the transformation of the heroine into a white mouse, and the eruption from the auditorium of the Stupid People, determined to have a happy ending at all costs.

When Prokofiev returned to Russia from the West he was delighted to find waiting for him a mass audience which was really interested in new music. His determination to write pieces which they could enjoy was an aesthetic, not a political, decision (for Prokofiev, interested in his own work to the exclusion of everything else, was perhaps the least political animal that ever lived). There is, therefore, in his Soviet works a tendency to concentrate — but without condescension — on the more approachable aspects of his musical character. Prokofiev was well aware of the problems involved: 'Nothing is more difficult to discover than a melody which would be immediately understandable even to the uninitiated listener, and, at the same time, be original. Here the composer is beset by numerous dangers; he is apt to become trivial or vulgar, or else dish out a repetition of something already heard before.' Despite this change in attitude, he continued, where appropriate, to indulge his taste for the grotesque (the music for the film *Lieutenant Kizhe*) and the aggressive (the wartime trilogy of piano sonatas). It is perhaps possible to discern the emergence of a sixth stylistic feature — a certain epic grandeur — in the works of the Soviet period. This can be heard at its

33

best in the choral prologue to the opera *War and Peace* and in the music for *Alexander Nevsky*; at its worst (though this is a minority opinion) in the very popular Fifth Symphony.

Propagandists of East and West would dearly love to use Prokofiev's creative career as an argument in favour of the superiority of their own system, but it cannot be done. His successes, like his failures — and both are to be expected from so prolific a composer — are evenly spaced throughout his life. Consider two late works, the Seventh Symphony and the Ninth Piano Sonata. The former, written (according to a Russian programme note) 'at the request of the Music Section of the Soviet Radio for children and youth', is a most grievous disappointment, whereas the latter is simultaneously a masterpiece of limpid lyricism and a highly ingenious treatment of the concept of cyclic form. (The main theme of each successive movement is, so to speak, pre-echoed in the coda of the previous one.) The best achievements of the European years all have Soviet parallels — the First Violin Concerto for instance, is matched by the second, and the last three piano concertos by the last four piano sonatas. Similarly, the stage successes previously mentioned have their Soviet counterparts in the ballet *Romeo and Juliet* and the opera *War and Peace*. (It is surely no coincidence that the most striking episode in the latter is also a dance sequence. After a ballroom scene involving the whole company the stage is suddenly vacated; alone under the spotlight Prince Andrew and Natasha meet each other for the first time, to the accompaniment of one of the most ravishing waltzes ever written by Prokofiev. Perhaps the only gift he had in common with Shostakovitch was the ability to take stereotypes like the waltz and the march and to make them the vehicle for highly personal utterances.)

* * *

Compared with Prokofiev, Shostakovitch was a late developer. This may seem an extraordinary statement in the light of the success of his First Symphony; but despite the originality and assurance of the thematic ideas, their formal treatment is purely conventional. It was only after its completion that Shostakovitch began to get to grips with a three-pronged problem: how to write a large-scale work which at one and the same time would express Soviet ideals, satisfy his own musical instincts, and present the resulting new sounds in a structurally convincing fashion. For this reason his next three attempts, though less successful, were in reality a step forward. No 2 ('October') starts with an impressionistic sketch of the dawn of revolution, in which polyrhythmic techniques are

34

used with stunning imagination. A broadly popular choral finale brings the one-movement design to an end in a blaze of C major and a series of shouted slogans; in between comes a keyless polyphonic web, redolent of Hindemith, involving at one point 13 independent parts. Not surprisingly, the overall impression is one of stylistic incoherence; but it is a very exciting piece for all that.

No 3 ('Mayday') is also a one-movement work with a choral finale, but there are four clearly demarcated sections corresponding to the traditional symphonic pattern. There are two unusual features: the deliberate rejection of thematic development, and the wordless oratory given (after the manner of Berlioz) to the trombones. The result is a realistic portrayal of the celebrations annually held in Red Square on the first of May, but does not succeed in being any less tedious to the Western observer than the event itself.

For his Fourth Symphony, Shostakovitch abandoned programmatic evocations of Party festivals, and for the first time in his symphonic writing succeeded in speaking unmistakeably with his own individual voice. The strident beginning of the work and the long lingering close are among his finest and most original pages, but the solution to the architectural problem still eluded him. The first movement sprawls self-indulgently; and the attempt, in the third, to incorporate within the same span a funeral march, a fast section and a dance *divertissement* ends in magnificent but predictable failure.

Little more than a year later, in 1937, Shostakovitch showed that he had learnt his last remaining lesson, self-discipline. The thematic material of the Fifth Symphony remains as personal, and is developed as resourcefully, as ever; what is new is the tautness and coherence of the structural design. Mastery of symphonic architecture had been Shostakovitch's aim ever since his graduation exercise of 1925, and he would certainly have achieved it sooner or later whatever the circumstances. But it is arguable, like it or not, that the process was hastened by the almost unbearably painful pressures to which he was subjected by the Party. To have had one's work described in *Pravda* as 'chaos instead of music' must, like the prospect of being hanged, have concentrated the mind wonderfully.

One of the by-products of the crisis was Shostakovitch's entry into the world of the string quartet. 'As you or I might find relaxation in listening to a quartet', wrote Hugh Ottaway, 'so did Shostakovitch in writing one.' The sunny mood of the work, its apparent simplicity and undoubted brevity, have led many critics to underestimate it. It can indeed be called Haydnesque, but only in the sense that Haydn would have been proud to acknowledge it. While Shostakovitch was mastering

35

the symphony and transferring that mastery to the world of the string quartet, he was also grappling with opera. *The Nose* contains enough brilliant ideas to establish the reputation of any young composer. Diaghilev would never have needed to ask him (as he asked Cocteau) to 'astonish me', since practically every bar is an astonishment in itself — not least the interlude for unaccompanied percussion. But a sense of dramatic timing is lacking. Scenes like the ambush laid by the police for the Nose at the coach-station are too long, whereas the ending is too abrupt. *Lady Macbeth of Mtensk* represents as great an advance over *The Nose* as did the Fifth Symphony over the Fourth. The satirical scenes are, if possible, even more hilarious, but are now contrasted with sustained passages of deeply-felt lyricism. Moreover, in Katerina, the composer has created a tragic heroine who compels an audience's belief and sympathy. The fact that *Lady Macbeth* was the chief target for the denunciations in *Pravda* probably accounts for Shostakovitch's failure to pursue an operatic career; but like Beethoven after *Fidelio* he never finally abandoned the idea of writing again for the stage. *Testimony* refers to his firm intention (never fulfilled) of basing an opera on Chekhov's story *The Black Monk*, and in 1941 he actually started work on a second Gogol satire, *The Gamblers*. In his enthusiasm for the text he made the mistake of setting it without cuts, so that it rapidly became 'unmanageable'. But the main reason given for stopping 'after ten pages' (actually three-quarters-of-an-hour's worth of music) was his inability to conceive of anyone caring sufficiently for either Gogol or himself to perform it. This was a piece of self-deception; it would be truer to say that what he had so far written was, by his own standards, scarcely worth performing.

For the next 20 years or so Shostakovitch lived a double life: the public figure writing symphonies and the private man composing string quartets.* Except for the Ninth, the symphonies are all epic in character. Deep seriousness tends to be relieved by almost demonic outbursts of gaiety. The scale is vast; but the composer's Dickensian fertility of thematic invention and his inexhaustible capacity for motivic and contrapuntal development are held in check by his unerring grasp of tonal architecture. Some are avowedly descriptive; but programmatic inspiration is never far away even from compositions which purport to be wholly abstract. (According to Volkov, the savagery of the scherzo of the Tenth was provoked by Stalin's tyranny.) The last two symphonies in the group, the Eleventh and Twelfth, are both concerned with

* Other major works of this middle period include the Piano Quintet (1940), the Second Piano Trio (1944), and the first of the concertos for violin (1947–8) and cello (1959).

revolutions; the former depicts the unsuccessful uprising of 1905, the latter the victory of Lenin in 1917. Does the fact that the Eleventh Symphony is a masterpiece and the Twelfth an abysmal failure arise from a natural tendency in the composer himself to sympathise with disaster rather than triumph, or had he by 1961 already become disillusioned with the Party and composed his portrait of Lenin out of an all-too-obvious sense of duty?

Of the corresponding string quartets the Second and Fifth have something of the same epic quality as the symphonies. The other three are more personal, and seem pre-occupied with the idea of innocence — perhaps the innocence of childhood. The coda of the Third Quartet looks back with nostalgia at a paradise which can never be regained; but the sixth (like the finale of the Piano Quintet) suggests that it may, after all, lie within our reach. This particular quartet, written in 1956, is a work of the ripest mastery. For the slow movement Shostakovitch employs passacaglia form — one that always seems to bring the best out of the composer. The opening of the work involves a witty deception worthy of Agatha Christie; it is impossible to deduce, at a first hearing, that the viola's 'till ready' on a crotchet D will be eventually unmasked as the mainspring of the whole movement. Throughout, the subtleties of modulation are a joy; so is the harmonic astringency of the cadence which ends each of the four movements (derived, by another piece of sleight-of-hand, from the first entry of the cello).

In 1960 a new period begins, ushered in by the Seventh Quartet. This is one of Shostakovitch's most bleak and concentrated works; written in memory of his first wife, Nina, it conveys unmistakably a deep sense of loss. It was followed almost immediately by the Eighth, a tragic commentary (with self-quotations) upon the main events of the composer's life. It would be satisfyingly tidy if one could describe the remaining quartets as a continuing descent into despair; and indeed the Fifteenth and last, a sequence of six contrasting adagios, is desolate almost beyond belief. But in fact there is a return to innocence throughout the Tenth Quartet, and even to triumph in the closing pages of the Twelfth. This latter work is an architectural marvel. Despite a superficial appearance of being divided into two sections, further analysis reveals it as consisting of several movements enclosed within each other like a series of Chinese boxes.

The Twelfth Quartet (and the numbering is surely significant) also reveals one of the chief obsessions of the composer's old age: fully chromatic themes which use all 12 semitones once only, but within a strictly tonal context (in this case D flat). Other features of this final period are a love of quotation, generally with some autobiographical significance; a preference for an off-hand (almost 'throwaway') type of thematic material, uninteresting in itself but offering wide scope for subsequent development; a fondness for the motif D E flat C B natural (the musical transliteration of his own initials); and an increasing preoccupation with the beauties of instrumental sound for their own sake, rather than as a vehicle for the composer's ideas.

Not surprisingly, these features can all be found in the last three symphonies, because by this time the private and public worlds have become one. Like Webster in T S Eliot's poem, Shostakovitch was much possessed by death, and this is the theme of the cycle of 11 songs for soprano, bass, string orchestra and percussion which the composer called (using the term in a Mahlerian sense) his Fourteenth Symphony. This, the only one of his symphonic works to lack a tonal resolution, is widely regarded as the summit of his achievement; but it is equalled by the five settings of Yevtuschenko for unison male voices and orchestra which comprise the Thirteenth and by the purely orchestral Fifteenth Symphony. In the latter a return to the earlier concept of innocence alleviates the composer's obsessive concern with death (they are represented by familiar quotations from Rossini and Wagner respectively); and in the last movement of both symphonies the grim fact of man's mortality is accepted with a simplicity and resignation which are deeply moving.

* * *

The progress of Shostakovitch from promise to maturity, and then, after a period of heroic challenge, to an acceptance of the limitations of the human condition, would seem in every way to parallel the development of Beethoven; and only critics unable to come to terms with their own century would claim that the musical achievement was inferior. Certainly the discipline, the introspection and the sheer beauty of sound to be found in the final works of both composers are of the same order. But there is one difference, as significant as it is obvious. For Beethoven, unorthodox though he was in much of his religious belief and practice, death was the gateway to life; for Shostakovitch it was the prelude to annihilation. This credo, implicit in the music, is explicitly stated in *Testimony*: 'Fear of death may be the most intense emotion of all. I sometimes think that there is no deeper feeling ... I fear death less now, or rather, I'm used to the idea of an inevitable end and treat it as such. After all, it's the law of nature and no-one has ever eluded it ... To deny death and its power is useless.' It was to be expected that Shostakovitch would cling to the atheistic beliefs in which he had been brought up; but in *Testimony* he is also represented as denying Christians the right to cling to theirs. Verdi is accused of a 'cowardly act' in refusing to acknowledge the finality of death at the end of *Otello*. This, if no fabrication, shows a lack of imagination extraordinary in so musically imaginative a composer.

It is this shallowness of mind (evident whenever topics other than music are discussed in *Testimony*) which raises doubts as to the accuracy of Volkov's reporting. Nobody mentioned in the book escapes censure; those who complied with Stalin's whims are pictured as snivelling cowards and bootlicking toadies (though no excuse is offered in extenuation of the composer's own acceptance of official honours). On the other hand, Solzhenitsyn and Sakharov are not to be trusted; and as for Yudina the pianist, who was brave enough to tell Stalin that she was giving the fee he had paid her to the Church and that she would be saying prayers for him, she was nothing but a crank. Abuse is not reserved solely for believers: Bernard Shaw and other 'famous humanists' come under fire for accepting the Soviet regime at its face value. Here a good case is spoilt by the failure to recognise the moral courage of those others like George Orwell and André Gide who, after seeing communism in action, readily admitted that their belief in a Marxist Utopia had been mistaken.

Volkov may have tried to paint a true portrait of Shostakovitch, but he would have served his sitter better by suppressing it. In any case, such truth as *Testimony* does contain is demonstrably incomplete. There was another side to the composer's character in old age, and this is revealed in his last public utterance — an open letter written on the occasion of UNESCO's first 'International Day of Music': 'Every genuinely profound musical work is the realisation of the thoughts and aspirations, not of a single person, but of many human beings. In the work of a really big musician one always hears the voice of his people. This is borne out by the work of Bizet, Verdi, Mussourgsky, Prokofiev, Bartók, Honegger, Lutoslawski, Britten ... in music, as in any other sphere of creative activity, it is absolutely imperative to master new ways. If art stopped developing, that would spell its end as a creative effort. That art today knows many ways of renovating itself is good and encouraging, but of these ways only those hold promise for the future that grow out of the great classical traditions ... We are often told today that the complexity of modern art can be explained by the fact that it is in the process of 'rearmament'. But have we the right to suspend the functioning of art "for over-hauling", thus depriving people, albeit temporarily, of their life's companion? The answer is an emphatic: No!'

These words come nearer to the essential nobility of Shostakovitch's music than anything to be found in Volkov.

PART II

6. Purcell and Dryden

In his own day Purcell's position must have seemed unassailable. 'He had a most commendable ambition of exceeding everyone of his time,' wrote his contemporary Thomas Tudway, 'and he succeeded in it without contradiction, there being none in England, nor anywhere else that I know of, that could come into competition with him for compositions of all kinds.' And yet within relatively few years of his death Purcell was relegated to the history books and all his music (except for a handful of songs and some mutilated anthems) had disappeared from the repertory. The counter-tenor voice beloved by the composer gave way to the imported castrato, the technique of baroque trumpet-playing fell into disuse, the orchestra was banished from church and the trio sonata was superseded by the string quartet. Moreover, manuscripts were mislaid and performing traditions forgotten. The Restoration stage, which had inspired most of the finest work of Purcell's last years, was first undermined by the attacks of Jeremy Collier (precursor of our contemporary crusader, Mary Whitehouse), and then destroyed by Walpole's political censorship. The entire musical climate changed beyond recognition; to Burney, the daring innovations of Purcell's teacher John Blow were explicable only in terms of ignorance of harmony or barbarity of taste; a generation later they ceased to be explicable at all.

It was left to the 20th century — like the 17th century, an 'age of anxiety' in the arts as well as in politics — to rebuild what had been destroyed. Singers, players, scholars and composers united in a campaign to rehabilitate Purcell's reputation. Long-lost instrumental and vocal techniques were rediscovered, authentic editions prepared, and performing practices elucidated. (Some of what has been learnt will, however, need to be unlearnt once the first excitement has abated. It is simply not credible that a craftsman as meticulous as Purcell should treat the dotting of one of a pair of quavers as a matter of indifference; nor should the absence of written ornamentation* be taken by performers as a direct incitement to decorate melodic lines regardless of either character or context.) As a result, the verdict of Corno di Bassetto, which must have sounded like a typical Shavian paradox when first pronounced

---

* Purcell was as aware as Rossini of the importance of notating ornamentation precisely: see the recitative *'Tis nature's voice* from the *St Cecilia Ode* of 1692.

in 1889 — 'Purcell was a great composer, a very great composer indeed' — is now everywhere accepted; everywhere, that is, save the one place where it is most deserving of acceptance, the opera house.

Critics of Purcell's major stage works (dismissively termed 'semi-operas') start from the premise that there is something irremediably wrong with their form. As a preliminary to challenging that assumption, it may be as well to recapitulate as briefly as possible the generally accepted view of the origins of Restoration opera. (Differences among historians are mainly a matter of emphasis.) The prime source — as of all opera — was the pioneering work of the Florentine Camerata, news of which was brought back to England by composers who had been trained in Italy, like Walter Porter and John Cooper (Coprario). A later foreign source was the French court ballet of Molière and Lulli. Here again there was direct contact between the countries involved; apart from musical exchanges, Restoration playwrights made it their business to be familiar with the latest developments in French drama. (It will be recalled that Pelham Humfrey, the most promising young English composer of the day, was transformed into an 'absolute Monsieur' as a result of studying abroad at the King's expense; while in his absence Charles imported Louis Grabu — a sort of 17th-century Pierre Boulez — to take charge of the royal orchestra.) The most important indigenous source was the Jacobean masque. These elaborate and costly entertainments were normally staged for one performance only by an aristocratic patron anxious to ingratiate himself with some high-ranking visitor. In them music, dancing (amateur and professional), poetry and scenic design met on roughly equal terms — despite Inigo Jones' attempt to have his name printed above Ben Jonson's on the poet's own title-page. Through-composed music (as in Nicholas Lanière's *Lovers made men*) seems to have been a rare exception. Finally, it should be remembered that there was a long established tradition of music in the 'straight' theatre; dramatists like Shakespeare used music not merely as a decoration but as a structural force. (The precise placing of the two songs in *Cymbeline* is a case in point. If, as sometimes happens, the dirge is spoken instead of being sung, a gap appears in the dramatic fabric and the play's delicate balance is destroyed.)

The circumstances attending the return to the throne of Charles II were exceptionally favourable for the creation of a specifically English type of opera. Even before the King's re-appearance D'Avenant had (after a trial run) successfully circumvented the Puritan ban on theatres with a combination of drama and music called *The seige of Rhodes*, on the pretext that the resulting performance was more musical than dramatic.

D'Avenant, it is true, returned to the legitimate stage as soon as circumstances permitted; but his fellow pioneer Matthew Locke continued to compose operas in collaboration with Thomas Shadwell and other librettists. Audiences were weary of the drab conformity of life under the Commonwealth, and ready for any kind of spectacular and colourful entertainment. In King Charles, anxious as he was to rival the splendours of Versailles, artists found the perfect patron (despite a weakness for distributing I.O.U.s rather than actual money). A continuing love of the dance was fostered by special schools, such as those of Luke Channell and (later) Josias Priest. Finally — a similar happy conjunction had occurred previously during the reign of Elizabeth I — a group of dazzling talents appeared on the literary scene just as Purcell's genius was reaching maturity. The plays of Congreve, Dryden, Vanbrugh, Wycherley (and later Farquhar) rank among the most brilliant in English theatrical history.*

The background to the birth of Restoration opera was such that it was not only logical but inevitable that it should take the form of an alliance of all the arts and not, as in Wagner, a fusion of them. Music, poetry, dance and spectacle combined to produce a totally integrated dramatic experience while at the same time retaining their own individual function and identity. In the case of music this was not difficult to define. Because of its supernatural associations music was clearly the province of gods, goddesses, fairies, demons and their earthly ministers, such as wizards and witches. Secondly, in the theatre, as in life, music was felt to be an essential accompaniment to all manner of ceremonial: regal, religious and military. Thirdly, there were some classes of human beings who because of their character and situation might reasonably be expected to indulge in music during the course of their everyday life: madmen — subsuming those who were temporarily insane, like lovers and drunks — and rustics. (In the preface to *Albion and Albanius*, Dryden justifies the inclusion of the latter with amusingly urban naivety: 'and therefore Shepherds might reasonably be admitted, as of all Callings, the most innocent, the most happy, and also by reason of the spare Time they had in their almost idle Employment ...' Dryden was indeed correct in regarding countryfolk as natural singers; but their songs — like those of sailors and convicts — were the product not of leisure but of unremitting hard work.)

There is nothing nonsensical about all this. On any objective view

---

* For more detailed information see E. J. Dent: *Foundations of English Opera*. The role of Matthew Locke has recently been reassessed by Murray Lefkowitz (R.M.A. Proceedings, vol. 106).

Dryden's aesthetic theory is more valid than that of Wagner (of whose tautological approach Debussy so rightly complained), and more realistic than the *verismo* of Puccini. Support for Dryden is forthcoming from an unexpected quarter: an essay entitled 'The future of opera' by Ferrucio Busoni (Berlin, 1913). 'At what moments is music indispensable on the stage?' he asks, and replies to his own question with the words 'during dances, marches, songs, and at the *appearance of the supernatural in the action*' (my italics). A little later he declares: 'The opera should take possession of the supernatural or unnatural as its only proper sphere of representation and feeling and should create a pretence world in such a way that life is reflected in either a magic or a comic mirror, presenting consciously that which is not to be found in real life … And dances and masks and apparitions should be interwoven, so that the onlooker never loses sight of the charms of pretence or gives himself up to it as an actual experience'.

Broadly speaking, two choices were open to a Restoration librettist. He could either construct his own scenario, making the opportunities for musical scenes arise naturally out of the plot, or he could take an existing play (preferably one already involving magic) and expand those elements — supernatural, rural, and ceremonious — particularly suited to music. The latter course was adopted by Shadwell for *The Tempest* and by Elkanah Settle (if the identification is correct) for *The Fairy Queen*. Dryden preferred to create his own original plot; and if there are certain aspects of *King Arthur* which are unsympathetic to a modern audience, every detail of the story was calculated to appeal to the taste of the 17th-century theatre-goer. In seeking to combine within a single framework a ritual human sacrifice, a battle, a country idyll, a river scene, a patriotic pageant and the magical transformation of icy wastes into the kingdom of love, Dryden set himself a formidable problem. But the ingenuity of his solution could hardly have been bettered by John Dickson Carr.

Dryden had begun his operatic career under the delusion (still shared today by many of his countrymen) that only a foreigner was capable of composing music. Accordingly he selected Louis Grabu to collaborate in the writing of *Albion and Albanius*, although Purcell had already been working in the theatre for five years. But Grabu's chauvinistic ignorance, combined with the success of Purcell's music for Betterton's *Dioclesian*, made him change his mind. In the preface to his play *Amphitryon* (for which Purcell had supplied the incidental music), Dryden handsomely recanted, praising 'the excellent composition of Mr Purcell; in whose Person we have at length found an English Man, equal with the best abroad. At least my opinion of him has been such, since his happy and judicious performances in the late opera' (i.e. *Dioclesian*). When Dryden came to publish *King Arthur* he was (if possible) even more enthusiastic: 'There is nothing better, than what I intended, but the Musick: which has since arriv'd to a greater Perfection in *England*, than ever formerly; especially passing through the Artful Hands of Mr *Purcel*, who has Compos'd it with so great a Genius, that he has nothing to fear but an ignorant, ill-judging Audience.' Their partnership continued with *The Indian Queen* (in which a third participant was Dryden's brother-in-law, the playwright Robert Howard); this was Purcell's last* and arguably finest dramatic score, but also (sadly) an unfinished one. (The opera was completed after Henry's death by his brother Daniel, who supplied the missing music for the final masque with the maximum of efficiency and the minimum of inspiration.)

In praising Purcell so highly, Dryden could well be suspected of self-interest; but he spoke neither more nor less than the truth. Three of Purcell's most obvious merits as a dramatic composer — the vitality of his rhythms, the poignancy of his harmonies, and the spontaneity of his most complex as well as his simplest melodies — can be seen in close juxtaposition in the masterly scena 'Ye twice ten hundred deities' from *The Indian Queen*. The principal section, 'By the croaking of the toad', sweeps onward with irresistable energy, to be followed by one of those astonishing passages of chromatic harmony which suggests that Purcell was born 150 years ahead of his time. It will not escape notice that Purcell has achieved his imaginative ends by the most strictly logical of means:

---

* The greater part of *The Tempest*, once thought to be by Purcell, has been convincingly assigned to Purcell's pupil, John Weldon, by Dr Margaret Laurie (R.M.A. Proceedings, vol. 90). The thinness of texture in the choral passages, and the sequential symmetry of the solo vocal writing, conclusively disprove Purcell's authorship of the masque; though it contains some most beautiful music.

The whole scene (which is written with a singer's understanding of the human voice) ends with one of the most ravishing of the composer's melodies, set to the words:

> 'While bubbling Springs their Musick keep,
> That use to Lull thee in thy Sleep.'

In some other respects Purcell's supremacy is not self-evident. It is a truism that the best art conceals art, and so effortless does his music sound that it is easy to forget that Purcell had all the musical techniques of the day at his fingertips. Like Mozart, he retained a lifelong desire and ability to learn from others; so that on to the English musical tradition in which he was brought up, he was able to graft the latest ideas from France introduced by Pelham Humfrey, as well as those acquired from his own study of 'the most fam'd Italian masters'. Every kind of intellectual device can be found in his music, often (it would seem) undertaken simply for his own amusement and satisfaction, since there was no likelihood that they would be observed by many, if any, of his listeners. At the end of what Tudway calls 'the Freezing piece of Musick' in *King Arthur* there is a duet on the grandest scale for soprano and bass: 'Sound a parley, ye fair, and surrender'. By way of accompaniment Purcell has provided, instead of just the customary figured bass, a trio sonata movement for two violins and continuo which develops (along quite separate lines) the musical material given to the voices. The structure therefore consists not of one duet but two, proceeding independently yet simultaneously. Spectacular feats such as this (and there are many) are not the best evidence of Purcell's mastery; even more significant is his unremitting attention to detail. (Much of the rhythmic vitality already referred to is due to the contrapuntal independence of the inner orchestral parts.) The battle sequence in *King Arthur* includes a tiny but striking example. When the chorus take over from the soloist the words 'thundering drum', Purcell momentarily drives the basses above middle C with quite thunderous effectiveness:

thun – d'ring drum.

Detailed discussion of Purcell's skill in setting the English language to music seems hardly necessary, since the vitality of his declamation and the vividness of his pictorial imagination are now everywhere recognised. One point, however, needs to be made. No matter how elaborate the detail within a phrase, Purcell never loses sight of its overall shape and direction. Once begun, it drives straight as an arrow towards its target. One cannot do better than follow Holst's example and study the recitatives (which were such a revelation to him) in *Dido and Aeneas*. In the first scene, every nuance of Dido's account of the hero's career and character is captured in the music — which none the less sweeps unhesitatingly forward towards the final cadence so as to form a single unbroken melodic arch. In its very different way the declamation given to the witches in the second scene is also a miracle of subtle expressiveness. Consider the Sorceress' description of her plan to have Aeneas ordered to set sail *tonight*. The prolongation of the second syllable (like the drawing back of a bowstring) supplies a tremendous rhythmic impetus, while at the same time the upward leap of an octave gloatingly emphasises the cruelty of what is to be the final twist of the knife.

Indispensable to any composer of opera is an understanding of what another master has called 'the psychology of the individual'. Given the chance Purcell (like Mozart again) could create characters who live for us like real people. It is not just the poignancy of the music of her lament which moves us to tears: it is Dido herself. (It is perhaps less often remarked that in Aeneas Purcell sketched an extraordinarily lifelike portrait of a man who believes himself to be unshakeable, but is in fact forever changing his mind — drawn with a few rapid strokes in just a handful of bars of recitative.) But let us leave *Dido and Aeneas* on one side (for as a through-composed chamber opera it is not characteristic of his dramatic work as a whole) and turn to the finest of the Shakesperian adaptations, *The Fairy Queen*. In the first act Purcell portrays with devastating realism those sudden emotional *bouleversements* which we have all observed occurring to other people — though not of course ourselves — under the influence of alcohol. When the drunken poet is captured and hauled before Titania, he and the music lurch around in a state of magnificent euphoria: 'I'm drunk, boys, as I live, boys, drunk.' Ordered to admit his crimes he plunges — after a few carefree repetitions of the words 'I confess' — straight into the depths of despair with a suddenness that recalls the experience of William Mulliner after sampling straight rye in a speakeasy called Mike's Place. Only a dramatist of the widest sympathies could portray with equal fidelity and affection a tragic heroine and a drink-sodden hack.

Purcell's crowning glory is his ability to build a scene into a dramatic whole. Technically his methods are many and various: thematic development and repetition, contrasts of texture and tempo and (most importantly) the structural use of tonality. But underlying all these is his sense of dramatic momentum. The five masques which comprise the music for the five acts of *The Fairy Queen* all exhibit this sense, and none better than the nocturnal sequence in which Titania is entertained successively by Night, Mystery, Secrecy and Sleep. The leading parts are distributed between soprano, counter-tenor and bass soloists, with varied instrumental support (the upper strings muted; continuo alone; oboes obbligati, and full string orchestra). The prevailing tonality is C minor, with a digression (lest this should grow wearisome) into the relative major when Sleep and his attendants begin the final section. An extraordinarily mesmeric effect is produced here by Purcell's use of silence, and it is worth noting that the rests are not of uniform duration, but unequal. The masque ends with a dance set as a canon 4 in 2, as if Purcell wished to prove that the creation of a hypnotic atmosphere and the solution of an abstruse intellectual problem were (in his case) not incompatible tasks.

If the aesthetic basis of Dryden's operas is admitted to be defensible, and if the universality of Purcell's gifts are such that they have been surpassed only by those of Mozart and, in his old age, of Verdi*, what is the objection to reviving their operas? Primarily, one of expense; even the original company could make very little profit despite full houses. Purcell cannot be done on the cheap. Experienced actors and dancers, virtuoso singers and lavish decor are of the essence. (Among other things, the stage directions of *The Fairy Queen* call for a wood through which runs a river bridged by an arch of dragons; a Chinese garden; cascades of water feeding a fountain 12 feet high; and the descent of Phoebus in a chariot drawn by horses and of Juno in one drawn by peacocks.) Given the will, however, none of these demands are impracticable. The other main objection is that, like most multi-media projects, Restoration opera works well on paper but not in practice. Against this one can only set personal experience. Immediately after World War II Covent Garden was re-opened with a truncated version of *The Fairy Queen* directed by Constant Lambert. (Some Purcell, including the scene of the drunken poet, and most of Shakespeare were cut.) Even in its abbreviated form it was a dazzling theatrical evening — all the razzmatazz of Battersea Fun Fair allied to the most ravishing words and music. When at the Lisbon Festival some years ago Purcell was the 'featured' composer, a cast was flown over from London and the opera performed complete.

---

* The splendour of Wagner's genius is indisputable, but his range is not universal. There is nothing to laugh at in his dramas — certainly not the pitiable Beckmesser. 'Had he (Wagner) been a little more human, he would have been altogether great.' (Debussy: *Monsieur Croche*)

The producer (David William) reported that the overall effect was not merely colourful and exciting but *cumulative*; the closing masque of Hymen proved to be not the last in a series of disconnected episodes but a fitting climax to all that had gone before.

The musical theatre has never been exclusive. It has admitted opera with spoken dialogue on equal terms with Wagnerian music-drama, and has given house-room impartially to composers who tell their story solely through the dance and those who tell it solely through *bel canto*. It would seem, to say the least, a pity to exclude a form which embraces all these delights simultaneously. In our own day Handel and Monteverdi, at one time considered intractable material, have been successfully revived. Why not Purcell, who is, after all, our own — and no poor thing either?

7. David and Goliath II

By way of an introductory fanfare to the première of his realisation of Purcell's *Dido and Aeneas* at the Lyric Theatre, Hammersmith, on May 1st 1951, Benjamin Britten issued the following statement to the press:

> There is no original manuscript extant of *Dido and Aeneas* — not a note remains in Purcell's handwriting. The oldest manuscript that survives is in the library of St. Michael's College, Tenbury, and is probably early eighteenth century, which contains music to all the opera except for a passage at the end of Act II.
>
> Anyone who has taken part in, or indeed heard, a concert or stage performance, must have been struck by the very peculiar and most unsatisfactory end of this Act II as it stands; Aeneas sings his very beautiful recitative in A minor and disappears without any curtain music or chorus (which occurs in all the other acts). The drama cries out for some strong dramatic music, and the whole key scheme of the opera (very carefully adhered to in each of the other scenes) demands a return to the key of the beginning of the act or its relative major (ie, D*, or F major). What is more, the contemporary printed libretto (a copy of which is preserved in the library of The Royal College of Music) has perfectly clear indications for a scene with the Sorceress and her Enchantresses, consisting of six lines of verse, and a dance to end the act. It is my considered opinion that music was certainly composed to this scene and has been lost. It is quite possible that it will be found, but each year makes it less likely.
>
> It is to me of prime importance dramatically as well as musically to include this missing scene, and so I have supplied other music of Purcell's to fit the six lines of the libretto, and a dance to end in the appropriate key. It is interesting in this connection to note that in the 1840 edition published by the Musical Antiquarian Society, it was apparently thought impossible to end the act with a recitative and the difficulty was overcome by including the first two numbers of the next act, *i.e.*, the Sailors' song and dance.
>
> The realization of the figured bass for harpsichord is, of course, my own responsibility; in Purcell's time it was the custom for the keyboard player to work it out afresh at each performance. Therefore, no definitive version of this part is possible or desirable.

By making this pronouncement Britten turned what might have been regarded as a routine occasion into an event distinctly out of the ordinary

---

* D minor.

— a characteristic example of his managerial, as opposed to his musical, genius. All the same, I felt that the statement should not be allowed to pass without comment, if only because — apart from the stated intention to supply some supposedly missing music — it contained no information which had not been generally available for more than half a century.

To the Editor, The Times.

Sir, — The peculiar state of the end of Act II of Purcell's opera *Dido and Aeneas* noted by Mr Benjamin Britten will be familiar to anyone who has studied the Purcell Society's edition published many years ago. It is quite clear from the libretto that Nahum Tate had planned the scene to end with a chorus and dance: it is equally clear from the musical key-scheme that Purcell had intended to fall in with his proposal. What is not clear (and what Mr Britten does not explain) is how this one short musical section came to be lost when all the rest was carefully preserved. The most probable explanation is that it was deliberately destroyed by the composer himself. When the opera came to actual performance he must have found that Aeneas's solitary and heartbreaking recitatives made a far more effective ending to the act than the conventional witches' chorus previously planned, and the resulting excision was an undoubted stroke of genius. As for Nahum Tate, he seems to have anticipated Sheridan's Mr. Puff: 'To cut out this scene! — but I'll print it — Egad, I'll print it every word.'

The use of the word *carefully* — chosen (ironically enough) not to emphasise a point but to produce a better balanced sentence — proved to be a fatal exaggeration, and my slingshot passed harmlessly over Britten's head.

To the Editor, The Times.

Sir, — In his letter of May 3 Dr Geoffrey Bush states that Purcell's music to *Dido and Aeneas* has been 'carefully preserved'. That is not quite the case. The only surviving manuscript of the music seems to be one written by John Travers 25 years after the death of Purcell and 40 years after the only contemporary performance of the work. Travers was not born at the time of this performance, and judging by obvious copying errors in the manuscript he cannot have been very familiar with the work, and it can never have been used for performance. The source for Dr W H Cummings's Purcell Society edition was written 'probably in Purcell's time' (Dr Cummings's words). This came to light in the 1880s and has since disappeared (according to Professor E J Dent). It differs widely from the above Travers manuscript which is preserved in the library of St Michael's College, Tenbury. There was apparently yet another manuscript consulted by MacFarren for his edition of the work for the Musical Antiquarian Society in 1841, which again differs from the above version, actually being considerably shorter. It seems that there is no trace of this manuscript to-day. 'Carefully preserved' is, therefore, a scarcely accurate phrase to use.

The musical scheme of *Dido and Aeneas* is remarkable: each scene is a complete unit containing many numbers in closely related keys following each other without pause, and ending in the same tonality or its relative major or minor as it started in (very much like his own verse-anthems and sonatas in fact). That Purcell, as Dr Bush suggests, should suddenly at the last moment abandon this plan for one of the scenes seems to me inconceivable. For one thing, it is completely foreign to the aesthetic attitude of the time. For another, it suggests that he rated the part played by tonality in form as low as many composers do to-day. No, I am afraid that I accept the verdict of the one piece of contemporary evidence we have — the libretto — and judge that the work still remains, alas, incomplete. Until such a happy event as the discovery of the missing numbers occurs, I believe it is better to restore the original symmetry of the work with Purcellian material than to leave this wonderful musical building with a large hole in it.

Had I only known it, the perfect demonstration of the unreliability of a printed libretto as operatic evidence was ready to hand — in Britten's own work. Like Purcell, Britten had himself omitted many passages (and altered others) in the libretto of *Peter Grimes*; and like Nahum Tate, Montagu Slater had later published the original version in full. I owe this information to Eric Crozier, who (as first producer of *Peter Grimes*) was in at the birth of the opera. It would not have been easy to discover it unaided because of Slater's prefatory remarks, which are disingenuous to say the least: 'I have omitted some of the repetitions and inversions required by the music ... thus the present text is *to all intents and purposes the one to which the music was composed*' (my italics). Leaving aside the many minor alterations and omissions, Slater's text of Peter Grimes' two great monologues (in his hut, Act II scene 2, and on the beach, Act III, scene 2) bears little or no relation to what is sung in the opera. I ought, however, to have recalled for myself that Dryden was on record as being obliged to 'cramp his verses' when collaborating with Purcell on their opera *King Arthur*. If Purcell could dictate to a giant like Dryden, how much more ruthlessly would he not have been prepared to treat Nahum Tate, a vastly inferior poet?

Recently the tonal argument has also been destroyed, by Ellen Harris of Columbia University. In her book *Handel and the Pastoral Tradition* (OUP, 1980) she has convincingly demonstrated that the accepted sub-division of *Dido and Aeneas* into three unequal acts is as illogical as it is lopsided; properly considered, the opera falls into two symmetrical halves. On this analysis the hunting scene no longer appears as a self-sufficient entity; it is simply the opening section of the second act and as such does not require a completely circular key-scheme of its own.

Even if it were still felt necessary to return to D minor after the departure of the false Mercury and Aeneas' A minor apostrophe to the gods, Purcell himself provided a delightfully elegant expedient which does away with any necessity for recomposition. For this discovery I am indebted to yet another scholar, my friend and colleague Brian Trowell, King Edward Professor of Music at King's College, London. The hunting scene begins with a little prologue for strings entitled *Ritornelle*; what could be simpler or more suitable than to make it 'come round again' at the end in the guise of an epilogue? There need be no fear that repetition would produce an anti-climax; what was originally heard in the context of hope would now be heard in one of despair. In the hands of a master composer, formal recapitulation can so often produce subtly different emotional effects.

After relying so much on the expertise of others, I would like to add a footnote which, in the familiar phrase of Bertie Wooster's manservant, is a little thing of my own. Opera writers throughout the ages — for example, Mozart and da Ponte using *Non più andrai* as part of Don Giovanni's supper music — have always enjoyed an in-joke. It is my belief that Purcell and Tate were doing precisely that during this same hunting scene which we have been discussing. When Aeneas rejoins the ladies to display the trophies of the chase, he boasts of his success in a curiously convoluted manner:

> Behold, upon my bending spear
> A monster's head stands bleeding,
> With tushes far exceeding
> Those that did Venus' huntsman tear.

On the surface this is simply a nod in the direction of classical mythology; but I would like to think that the *cognoscenti* among Josiah Priest's audience were able to translate it and relish the real meaning underneath:

'John Blow's *Venus and Adonis* is dead; long live Henry Purcell's *Dido and Aeneas!*'

8. The harp at the party

'I am doatingly fond of music', Mrs Elton declared to Emma Wodehouse. 'Two carriages are not necessary to my happiness, nor are spacious apartments. But to be quite honest, I do not think I can live without something of a musical society. I condition for nothing else; but without music, life would be a blank to me.'

Nothing is more calculated to excite 20th-century derision than the passion of 19th-century Englishmen — and more especially Englishwomen — for making music. In the second most vulgar production of Shakespeare I have ever seen, a Victorian-dress version of *The Merchant of Venice,* Jonathan Miller sent the audience into hysterics by the simple expedient of having a Mendelssohnian duet sung by two extensive sopranos during — of all things — the casket scene. Such philistinism is surprising, since we have rarely amused ourselves at the expense of Victorian literature, and have long since ceased to laugh at neo-Gothic church architecture and the paintings of the pre-Raphaelites — with the exception, that is, of those who collected pre-Raphaelite paintings while they were still unconsidered trifles, and are now laughing all the way to the bank.

There are two reasons why people feel free to criticise the Victorian musical evening — that it consisted of rotten music rottenly performed. But will this verdict stand up to closer examination? Live performances, no matter how rotten they may be, take one to the very heart of music as none of our mechanically perfect recordings can — bogusly perfect, incidentally, since most of them consist of little bits of tape recorded separately and stitched together afterwards when the artists have left the studio. How wise E M Forster was to declare that though his own performances grew worse yearly 'never will I give them up. They compel me to attend — no wool-gathering or thinking myself clever here — and they drain off all non-musical matter. Playing Beethoven, as I generally do, I grow familiar with his tricks, his impatience, his sudden softness, his dropping of a tragic theme one semitone, his love, when tragic, for the key of C minor, and his aversion to the key of B major.' This *physical approach* to Beethoven, as Forster called it, is utterly unobtainable by sitting on one's behind in front of the latest product of the hi-fi industry. J B Priestley is another author who has pleaded guilty to distributing handfuls of wrong notes during domestic performances of chamber music, yet 'bestriding the hacked corpse of poor Smetana, I drank the milk of paradise'.

But, you will say, the Victorian amateur, unlike Forster and Priestley, performed mostly rubbish. This is quite untrue. Quartet parties played the works of Haydn, Mozart and Beethoven, singers tackled the madrigals of Morley and Marenzio. But even if it *were* true, in what way would this make the Victorians different from any other generation, except in kind? *They* produced sentimental rubbish, the baroque era produced boring and repetitive rubbish, and our own age produces trendy and (if Hans Keller is to be believed) unmusical rubbish. If the work of remoter ages seems to be of consistently higher quality, this is an illusion. Normally the good and the less good perish during the sifting process of history, and only the best survives. Even so, the ayres of the Elizabethan Thomas Whythorne still exist to prove that 'downright bad music' could be written during the sixteenth century. In Ernest Walker's opinion Whythorne's songs are 'as miserably feeble rubbish as can be imagined.'

But, I repeat, Victorian rubbish was sentimental, and that was its real crime. We are told that strong men wept openly in the streets when they heard that Dickens had killed off Little Nell; this would be impossible in a sternly realistic age like our own which houses the arts in concrete penitentiaries laughingly called the Hayward Gallery and the Queen Elizabeth Hall. Invisible 'no weeping' notices hang alongside the visible 'no smoking' ones inside our concert halls and serious theatres. Only in the commercial cinema are both vices reluctantly permitted. Or so we like to think. We are, of course, deceiving ourselves. Like the hardboiled private eyes of Hammett and Ross Macdonald, our tough exterior conceals a centre as soft and sickly as marzipan. Consider Henze's recent opera *We come to the river.* After two acts full of blindness, baby-killing and bloody revolution the work ends with a starry-eyed vision of a Utopian future; the cast kneel reverently behind the plastic mock-up of a baby while a spotlight sheds a celestial glow round the infant martyr to the proletarian cause. Henze and his librettist, Edward Bond, persuade us to take this 20th-century Little Nellery seriously by surrounding it with an enormously complex pseudo-intellectual apparatus: split stage-levels, three orchestras, a percussionist's conjuring act and a great deal of naive political philosophising. Dickens — himself a one-time opera librettist — would have given it us neat. The Victorians enjoyed their sentimentality openly and unashamed, whereas we need first to square it with our Puritan conscience. Our approach to emotion is so unhealthily furtive that we could well be called the dirty mackintosh brigade of music.

56

I would like to suggest two correctives to our current disapproval of Victorian music — less ignorance and more imagination. Imagination, though desirable, is not *essential* to the appreciation of early music, since it is obvious that people who lived, talked and dressed so very differently from us must have had different ideas about the arts. We have only to look at a portrait of a bewigged Dr Boyce to be in the mood to accept the formal symmetries and repetitions which delighted the Georgians, though we have long since dispensed with such things ourselves. We tolerate the interminable plays on words indulged in by supposedly witty characters in Shakespeare's comedies as a convention of the time, just as we accept the codpieces on their costumes. The Victorians, however, with their sober suits and hairy face, do not seem sufficiently removed from us to entitle them to have an aesthetic different from our own. But different it is, and equally valid. What is more, performing problems calling for scholarly solutions exist in the music of Queen Victoria's reign exactly as they do in that of Charles II's. Balfe's vocal cadenzas need 'realising' every bit as much as Purcell's figured basses. Only imagination will keep such facts fresh in the mind.

For the rest, we might remember that almost all the features of our musical life on which we pride ourselves had their beginning in the 19th century. It always astonishes me that people who talk glibly about a 20th-century renaissance of British music forget that any sort of birth involves a pregnancy. It was the despised and rejected English Romantics who pioneered public chamber concerts and sonata recitals, fostered a love of J S Bach, made the first attempts to launch an English National Opera, founded the Philharmonic Society and our first two conservatories, made the widespread dissemination of music possible through popular publishing, and led the way in musicology with the first scholarly editions of the works of Purcell and Byrd. Some of these enterprises we may have improved upon, but none of them did we initiate, and one at least, popular publishing, we have virtually extinguished. As to British composers of the Victorian era, our ignorance of their music is perhaps excusable since so little is currently available in print. But Musica Britannica is planning to follow up its volumes of Field and Sterndale Bennett with four devoted to 19th-century songs; armed with these* it should soon be possible to take a view of our Victorian composers compounded of rather less Pride and Prejudice than it is at present.

---

* *English Songs 1800–1860* (the first of the series) was published in 1979.

9. The Silver Age of unaccompanied choral music

During my student days at university it was an article of faith that the English madrigal school had died under Cromwell, was buried during the Restoration, and remained securely under ground until Edmund Fellowes brought about its glorious resurrection between the years 1913 and 1924. A minimum of investigation is enough to show that this picture is quite untrue. Madrigals by English *and* European masters of Tudor and early Stuart times continued to be republished and regularly performed throughout the 18th and 19th centuries (a fact which Fellowes himself readily acknowledged). Small wonder that all through this period composers thought of the madrigal not as something archaic but as very much a going concern. In the best of their works pastiche is quite absent: the technique is madrigalian but the voice is the composer's own. Nothing, for example, could be more typical of the 18th century than Thomas Linley's five-part madrigal *Let me, careless*. Linley was born in 1732; he made his reputation in his home town of Bath, where he was a friend of Gainsborough, and then moved to London, becoming the chief composer and director of opera at the Drury Lane Theatre until shortly before his death in 1795. His family was even more musical than he; according to Roger Fiske, his daughter Elizabeth was one of the finest singers of the century until marriage put an end to her professional career, and his son Tom was as great a prodigy as Mozart (an opinion shared by Wolfgang Amadeus himself). Alas for promises; young Linley was drowned in a boating accident at the age of 22, before his superb gifts as violinist and composer could mature into something really great. So ended Linley senior's chance of going down to history as another Leopold Mozart; not, however, before he had collaborated with his son in providing the music for *The Duenna* (far and away the most noteworthy successor of *The Beggar's Opera*) to a text by Elizabeth's husband Sheridan. It is not without significance that in the course of the borrowing that was customary at the time he went to a madrigal composer, Thomas Morley, for the musical material of the finale.

A handful of Silver Age madrigals have survived into modern times — notably William Beale's ballet *Come let us join the roundelay* — and one single name, that of Robert Pearsall, who lived from 1795 to 1856. Pearsall was a Gloucestershire man, and one of the first members of the Bristol Madrigal Society, which dates back to 1837. In his later years (having left his wife) he settled with his daughter in a castle on the shores of Lake Constance. In this self-imposed exile he lost neither his enthusiasm for the English choral tradition nor for Gloucestershire. He published a considerable number of madrigals and other vocal works, always signing them in a way that sounds slightly comical to our 20th-century ears: Robert Lucas de Pearsall, Esquire, of Willsbridge. The best of his choral music has always been much admired by those familiar with it. Ernest Walker called his madrigals 'fully as musical as anything since Purcell ... exceedingly musicianly and vitalised work, with a very real air of distinction about them', and singled out for special commendation the eight-part setting of *Lay a garland on my hearse*: 'a most beautiful stately thing'. Massive sounds and complex textures seem to have appealed to Pearsall. The only work of his in general circulation, his version of *In Dulci Jubilo*, is in eight parts; his ballet *Sing we and chant it* is also in eight (though a weaker alternative version exists for half that number), and his *Ballad of Sir Patrick Spens* is in ten. But anyone who doubts Pearsall's ability to handle with equal assurance a simple four-part texture has only to look at the ballet *Shoot, false love* or the enchanting madrigal *Sweet as the flowers in May*. Incidentally, a comparison of the texts of these as given in the published edition and the composer's original manuscript in the British Library shows that Pearsall was a painstaking critic and corrector of his own work — not necessarily, however, always to its advantage.

Where would madrigals have been sung during the Silver Age? Not so much in private homes as in gatherings which were a cross between a convivial dining-club and a male-voice choral society. One such was the Noblemen and Gentlemen's Catch Club, which began operations in 1761. Its title was no idle boast. Among the founders were three earls and two generals, while the future George the Fourth was elected to membership in 1784, hotly followed in succeeding years by half-a-dozen dukes. Rather less Society-conscious was the Glee Club, which first met on December 22nd, 1787, at the Newcastle Coffee House, Castle Street, in the Strand. It removed to the Crown and Anchor in 1788, to the Freemason's Tavern in 1790 and back again to the Crown and Anchor in the following year, meeting and dining on alternate Saturdays. By 1814 the membership stood at 30, plus 13 professional singers who were honorary members of the Club, and four perpetual visitors. The Secretary of the Glee Club at this time, Richard Clark, has left us an account of the protocol observed at these meetings, of which there were ten each season. 'The hour of dining is half-past 4 o'clock, and the members take their seats at the table according to seniority, except the professional gentlemen, who always take their places in the centre of the table on each side. Each subscriber pays seven guineas for his ten nights, and is entitled to introduce one visitor on alternate nights, which visitor pays one pound'. The conjunction of wine and song, and the absence of women, is of course nothing new in our musical history; both were thoroughly approved of by Purcell and his contemporaries. The Victorians saw things rather differently; by 1857 the Glee Club had been dissolved and larger, fully amateur mixed-voice choirs were being formed, devoted solely to the study of music. Such groups were possibly wiser, probably sadder, certainly soberer, and undoubtedly more unwieldy. Simpler music was required for them, and it is from this moment that the partsong began to wax and the madrigal to wane. They had existed alongside for as long as anyone could remember; even in the madrigal's greatest days the four-part ayre had an honourable place in music-making, and the Victorian partsong is in direct line of descent from Dowland's set of 1597. A tremendous stimulus to the composition of partsongs was given by the success of Samuel Webbe's *Glorious Apollo* in 1790. Described quite inaccurately by the composer as a glee, *Glorious Apollo* is an undoubted partsong, and for 67 years from the date of its first performance enjoyed the distinction of being the first piece to be sung after dinner at every meeting of the Glee Club. From 1790 onwards partsongs appear more and more frequently in published collections of choral music. Many of them, despite the inevitable reduction in counterpoint content, are very fine, and none more so than the many Shakespearian settings of R J S Stevens, organist (simultaneously) of the Temple Church and the Charterhouse. He was also at one time Gresham Professor of Music; but nothing less academic than his five-part scherzo *It was a lover and his lass* can be imagined.

Two other forms which continued to be popular well into the 19th century remain to be discussed: the catch and the glee. Opinions differ about the derivation of the word catch. One possibility is that it comes from the Italian *caccia*, in hunting style; another, that it refers to the way each singer has to '*catch up* his part when the moment arrives' like a baton in a relay-race. William Barrett, however, the 19th-century researcher into such matters, explains that 'the melodies are so contrived by the composer that the sense of the words is changed from the original signification by the manner in which the singers appear to *catch at* each other's words'. In short, a catch is a kind of musical pun; on paper the text has one meaning, in performance quite another. As an example, consider *Holy Matrimony*, written by a cellist and minor composer of the 18th century, Stephen Paxton. The words read like a public-relations hand-out for a marriage bureau:

> A wife, o gods, how blest the man Who marries, ay, when'er he can.
> A curse attends the thoughtless drone Who dares to spend his days alone.
> A devil or a dev'lish fool Is he who loves alone to rule.

When sung, however, the juxtaposition of the first noun in each line — wife, curse, devil — puts quite a different complexion on the matter, producing the musical equivalent of Mr Punch's advice to those about to marry: don't.

One of the most ingenious punsters of the late 18th century was John Wall Calcott, oboeist, organist, composer, theorist and lecturer — everything by turns but nothing long. In order to encourage composers to enlarge the choral repertory, the Catch Club had (in 1763) instituted a series of annual prize competitions. In 1785 Calcott, in one of his periodic bursts of energy, presented the judges with nearly one hundred entries. A rule was immediately introduced to put a stop to such misplaced industry; this did not prevent Calcott in 1787 from carrying off all four prizes — a feat roughly the equivalent of Jim Laker's 19 wickets in the Manchester Test Match of 1956. Calcott's *Ah, how Sophia* is a poem to a faithless mistress:

> Ah, how Sophia can you leave Your lover, and of hope bereave?
> Go, fetch the Indians borrowed plume, Yet richer far than that you bloom.
> I'm but a lodger in your heart, And more than me, I fear, have part.

Or is it? Try repeating to yourself 'Ah, how Sophia' rather quickly several times. Yes, the real subject is a *house-a-fire*, and it is up to the lodger not to fetch Indians but fire-*engines*. Fire also plays a part in Calcott's equally preposterous joke *The Historians*. 1776 was the year which saw the publication of the first two histories of music in the English language (one complete, the other a first instalment). Calcott's glee shows us the admirers of Sir John Hawkins shouting at his rival 'Burney's history! Burn his history!'

Collections of catches were first published as long ago as 1609 by Thomas Ravenscroft. John Playford followed in 1651 and John Hilton the younger in 1652. Its capacity for double meanings — and the filthier the better — made the catch exceedingly popular in Restoration times; no doubt that is why the Purcell Society publishes the Master's work from an address in Soho. Later generations were not amused. In the 18th century, William Jackson of Exeter defined the catch a piece 'which, when quartered, had ever three parts obscenity to one part music'; in the 19th, a blushing William Barrett deplored the way in which 'the old spirit of harmless drollery was sacrificed for humour of a baleful and contaminating character.' Disapproval had an economic as well as a moral basis. Half a composer's customers were the wrong sex for this sort of hard-core material, so in 1778 Samuel Webbe published his first collection under the title: 'The Ladies Catchbook, being a collection of Catches, Canons and Glees, the words of which will not offend the nicest delicacy.'

But it is possible to be both nice *and* indelicate if you are clever enough, and Thomas Arne satisfies both conditions in his catch *The Interrupted Assignation*. The first voice to enter is John the servant, who is trying to seduce Jenny the maid. Jenny is the second singer: she threatens to cry 'Murder', but without any great conviction. Finally their mistress is heard, too crippled by gout to catch the culprits, but fully apprised of what is going on upstairs:

> My stars! What a noise! — and just over my head!
> Again! And Again! 'Tis the creak of the bed.

It would be a mistake to suppose that this type of canonic composition was necessarily humorous in intention — though the more serious variety was usually distinguished by the title round rather than catch. John Stafford Smith (of whom more later) chose the form for his passionate and moving elegy on the death of his fellow Glee Club member, the Duke of Cumberland. Some rounds and catches have a genuine lyrical inspiration — particularly those of Calcott's son-in-law, William Horsley. Horsley was born in 1774, and had the misfortune to study music under one Theodore Smith, who is tersely dismissed by Barrett as 'a musician of mean capacities and brutal mind.' Happier things were to follow; Horsley became a close personal friend of Mendelssohn, helped to found the Philharmonic Society in 1813, edited William Byrd's *Cantiones Sacrae* for the Antiquarian Society, and became the leading English composer of secular choral music of his generation. Three symphonies and piano sonatas await the attention of future researchers; meantime, *Rest, gentle youth*, a pastoral catch for four voices, and longer pieces like the madrigal *Why, gentle Shepherd on the mountain's brow* should be immediately restored to the unaccompanied choral repertory.

The generation before Horsley was dominated by Samuel Webbe, composer of *Glorious Apollo* and of *Would you know my Celia's charms*, one of the few catches that has never been forgotten. Webbe was born in Minorca in 1740; on settling in London he became organist of the Sardinian Embassy Chapel, for which he wrote a good deal of Roman Catholic church music. In 1787 he was appointed librarian of the Glee

Club, and in 1794 secretary of the Catch Club. By the time of his death in 1816 he had won, in the annual competitions, a record number of 27 prize medals — the 27th, by a coincidence that must have pleased him, in the same year that his son, Samuel Webbe junior, won his first. Such spare time as he had Webbe devoted to the study of six languages: Latin, Greek, Hebrew, French, German and Italian. Within the narrow limitations of partsong, catch and glee his music has remarkable variety; he never falls below a certain standard of craftsmanship and often rises a good deal higher. His five-part catch *The Riot* illustrates yet another aspect of the form; it can portray scenes of contemporary life with a Hogarthian vigour and fidelity. Webbe's subject here is the Gordon Riots of 1780, when Protestant mobs led by Lord George Gordon destroyed Roman Catholic chapels and private houses, set Newgate Gaol on fire and released the prisoners. As in sectarian Ireland today, troops had to be called out to deal with the rioters, and the severest penalties were imposed on all the ringleaders except Lord George himself. Dickens, incidentally, used these riots as the background of his novel *Barnaby Rudge.*

Glee is usually derived from the Anglo-Saxon word meaning music; and one of the earliest terms applied to guilds of musicians in this country was *Gleemen.* As the title for a choral composition it goes back at least as far as the 17th-century publications of John Playford, though perhaps it was not until the 18th that its requirements became strictly defined. The glee proper is a composition for unaccompanied solo voices, all male; it falls into several linked movements, with harmony predominating over counterpoint. In some ways, as Ernest Walker points out, it is a compromise between ayre and madrigal — more melodious and rhythmical than the latter, but more polyphonic than the former, and with a continuous, non-strophic design. It is a form peculiar to English music, and of course relies on that English vocal speciality, the counter-tenor. It was permissible, on occasion, to write parts above the counter-tenor, in which case these would be sung by boy trebles.

With the passing of time the term glee ceased to be strictly applied — in fact, by the end of the period it could be found on the title page of practically any piece of choral music, even the orchestrally-accompanied operatic choruses of Sir Henry Bishop. This of course, like our random use of the word symphony today, is the purest Humpty Dumpty-ism. ('When I use a word', said Humpty Dumpty, 'it means just what I choose it to mean — neither more nor less.')

John Stafford Smith's setting of Milton's *Blest Pair of Sirens* for five voices, including two trebles, shows the form at its best. Stafford Smith lived from 1750 to 1836; he was a choirboy at the Chapel Royal (where later he himself became Organist and Master of the Children), and a pupil of Boyce. He could be described as the father of English musicology, though I believe doubts have been expressed in American circles as to whether such a thing exists. At any rate, he supplied Sir John Hawkins with a number of transcriptions for his history, and himself published in 1779 an edition of English songs dating from around 1500, and, in 1812, two volumes of *Musica Antiqua*. His own music will never be forgotten as long as our American friends continue to perform *The Star-spangled Banner*, for the tune has been lifted from Stafford Smith's *Anacreon in Heaven*.

His setting of *Blest Pair of Sirens* falls into five sections. The first, which involves two tempo changes, expresses Milton's opening words in a splendidly declamatory fashion. The second moves at a gentle, regular pace and is descriptive of the 'undisturbed song of pure content' which is for ever sung in heaven. Next comes the central allegro, a brilliant choral depiction of the trumpets of the bright seraphim. More rapid tempo changes follow to illustrate the words 'disproportion'd sin', 'jarr'd against nature's chime' and 'perfect disapason', a phrase which is given, symbolically, to all five voices singing in octaves. This fourth section ends on a dominant pedal in the key of F sharp minor. The last movement, complete in itself, is a gentle air in triple time which is sung through twice. Compared with the massive climax of Parry's choral and orchestral setting of the same words, Stafford Smith's ending may seem self-effacing to a degree; yet in its context it is entirely satisfying and the glee as a whole (granted the form's limitations) is surely a miniature masterpiece.

10. Sterndale Bennett: the solo piano works

'Bennett is a pianist above all things' wrote Schumann. Of his compositions with opus numbers, nineteen are for piano solo and a twentieth is for piano duet. There are a further seven piano solos without opus number. He also published five concertante works for piano and orchestra, discarded a sixth and postponed publishing a seventh. The three chamber works all employ a piano, and the first of these, the Sestet op. 8, is virtually an eighth piano concerto with string accompaniment; indeed a manuscript copy of 36 bars of this work, at one time in the possession of Kellow J. Pye, actually bears the title Concerto.*

At the present time all these compositions are virtually unknown. Why? Chiefly, I think, because later generations have been content to accept the verdict of Guilty but Insane passed on Bennett by his immediate successors, without giving themselves the trouble of examining the only valid evidence — the works themselves. There are five main counts on the charge-sheet: (a) that Bennett was English, (b) that he was a Victorian, (c) that he wrote an oratorio *The Woman of Samaria*, (d) that he was Professor of Music at Cambridge, (e) that he was an inferior imitator of Mendelssohn.

Only to the first of these accusations can Bennett offer no defence. Certainly for the last two hundred years Englishmen have considered it a great crime for one of their fellow-countrymen to be a composer, and have showed their displeasure by making it as hard as possible for the thing to be done at all. If you think that matters have recently improved in this respect, try it yourself and see. Please do not attempt to refute this by pointing out that at the present time Tippett is widely (and justly) acclaimed. The same was true of Elgar, Delius, Holst and Vaughan Williams in their lifetimes (and, if it comes to that, Sterndale Bennett), but that did not prevent our local bulldozers from doing a ruthless job of demolition the moment these masters were safely dead and buried.

I am hopeful that to be a Victorian will shortly no longer be an automatic bar to serious consideration. We are slowly and painfully

---

* The source of this and other information about Sterndale Bennett is J R Sterndale Bennett's life of the composer (Cambridge, 1907). Quotations from Schumann are taken from his *Music and Musicians*, tr. Ritter (London, n.d.).

learning to love St Pancras Station and Keble College, Oxford; why not their musical equivalents? Similar re-assessments are occurring all the time; it is not so very long ago that the masterpieces of seventeenth-century English chamber music were summarily dismissed as drowthy aberrations. Certainly the first thing a musical Betjeman will point out is that Bennett deserves praise rather than blame for writing *The Woman of Samaria*, just as Caesar is to be praised rather than blamed for cutting off the hands of his defeated opponents after the seige of Uxellodunum; whereas all their contemporaries committed that sort of crime a hundred times, they did it only once.

To refute the notion that Bennett is an inferior imitator of Mendelssohn, it is only necessary to recall that once upon a time (it seems incredible) Arne was considered an inferior imitator of Handel. The parallel is almost exact; Mendelssohn (like Handel) is a major master, Bennett (like Arne) a minor one; neither Englishman can rise to the supreme heights of their rivals at their best; Bennett certainly never sank to the depths of Mendelssohn at his worst. Above all, there is an individual quality common to the music of both Englishmen, difficult to describe in words but unmistakable none the less; this is partly a matter of transparency of texture, partly a matter of lyrical spontaneity and freshness of inspiration.

If we wish to make a less superficial investigation of Bennett's musical ancestry, it will be necessary to go back to Mozart and even Domenico Scarlatti. The whole question is most ably dealt with by Schumann in his review of Bennett's *Suite de Pièces*, opus 24:

> The resemblance of his compositions to those of Mendelssohn has often been remarked; but those who think they have sufficiently designated Bennett's character by such a remark do him great injustice, and betray their own want of judgement. Resemblances are common between different masters of the same epoch. In Bach and Handel, in Haydn, Mozart and Beethoven in his earlier period, we find a similar aim, like a bond of union between them, which often expresses itself, as though one were calling unto the other. But this inclination of one noble mind to another should never be misnamed imitation.

In a previous article Schumann acknowledges a 'remarkable family resemblance' between the works of Bennett and Mendelssohn, but after listing several virtues common to both — 'beauty of form, poetic depth yet clearness, and ideal purity' — he adds significantly 'but with a difference'.

Since I am relying on Schumann's evidence as an expert witness, I must make a brief digression here to defend Schumann himself against his detractors. The argument against Schumann usually runs as follows: Bennett is a bad composer — Schumann praises him — therefore Schumann is a bad critic.* Professor Westrup denounces Schumann's review of Bennett's 3rd Piano Concerto as 'hopelessly exaggerated'. But Bennett as a young man was a prodigy both as composer and pianist, fully mature at the age of 16; to express astonishment 'at the early dexterity of this artist hand' strikes me as (if anything) an understatement. Bennett was universally regarded as a man of notable integrity, devoted to music as music, not as a source of self-advancement. How can Schumann be other than correct in asserting that were there many artists with the same qualities, 'all fears for the future progress of our art would be silenced'?

A re-reading of his collected articles shows Schumann to have been a shrewd as well as a generous critic. He had a gift for talent-spotting amounting almost to genius in itself, but he was a fearless enemy to anyone (Meyerbeer, for instance) whom he suspected of meretriciousness. Evidence of his perspicacity can be found in an unexpected and unimpeachable quarter. When Schumann first heard Wagner's *Tannhäuser* he found fault with the proportions of the second finale; and Wagner tells us (in *My Life*) that this was the precise place where he had been compelled to make a cut 'much against his own inclination'.

I have saved until last the consideration of Bennett's professorship. It is a curious thing that whereas a great keyboard virtuoso may be awarded a chair without anybody being so foolish as to suppose that his right (or left) hand has forgotten its cunning, a composer is liable to be written off immediately as a senile academic. Fortunately the rights and wrongs of this matter are irrelevant in Bennett's case. He had two quite distinct careers which to all intents and purposes never overlapped, and we can consider his achievements in the one field without the slightest reference to the other. A few dates will make this clear. Bennett was born in April 1816. He studied at the Academy from 1826 to 1836; but we may reckon that his career as a composer began in 1832, when he was 16, with the Piano Concerto in D minor, opus 1. A second period begins when he left the Academy in July 1836. During the next eight years he paid three visits to Germany, and reached the height of his powers as a composer. Dating the end of this period is a somewhat arbitrary business; some would put it at the end of his third visit to

---

* An article in the *Musical Times* for June 1964 by Gerald W Spink seems (if I have understood it correctly) to contain an ingenious variant of this argument: Bennett is a bad composer — Schumann is a good critic — therefore Schumann didn't praise Bennett as much as we all imagined.

Germany in 1842; I prefer 1844, the year of his marriage. At this point the break occurs: from 1844 until 1856 he was a free-lance teacher, conductor and concert-organiser; a very occasional pianist and a still more occasional composer. Those few short pieces he did write, either for pupils or on commission, seem mostly to have been done on 'the one day he stopped at home for his annual cold'. (The exception was a Sonata-Duo for cello and piano, written for one of his own chamber concerts; but this had to be completed between bouts of teaching in such feverish haste that although he had stayed up all the previous night to finish it, the work was still not ready when the soloist called to rehearse it two hours before the concert.)

Any ideas he had of resuming a creative career were ended by his election to the Cambridge Professorship in March, 1856. The final period, from then until his death in 1875, differs from the previous period only in that he was now a public teacher instead of a private one.

Why did Bennett give up being a composer at the age of 28? The main reason is obvious — the necessity of earning enough money to support a family. Bennett's tragedy was that, although by all accounts one of the finest pianists in Europe, he could not do this by playing if he remained in England, but only by the endless drudgery of teaching. Bennett was a man born out of due season. He did not choose to expend his gifts on flashy potpourris, for which there was a certain vogue at that time; apart from this there was only the occasional concerto date, and the chamber-music concerts which he organised himself at his own risk. It is extraordinary to note that when he played his *Musical Sketches* in Leipzig in 1842 at the age of 25, this was the first time he had ever played the piano in public without orchestral accompaniment.

Undoubtedly the three visits he paid to Germany between 1836 and 1842 must have been a tremendous stimulation and encouragement to him; how much more must he have felt *dis*couraged when he finally returned to philistine England, where a composer not only had no hopes in the present but (as far as he could see) no roots in the past. It is, I think, insufficiently recognised that researches undertaken in this century by British musicologists, besides being of incalculable value in themselves, have been a major factor in the revival of composition in England during this century. The links between Tippett and Purcell, Holst and Weelkes, Maxwell Davies and Taverner, are not fortuitous. A composer, in T S Eliot's words, needs 'a perception, not only of the pastness of the past, but of its presence'. Tippett himself says the same: 'more than anyone else, the creative artist needs a sense of continuity'. No composer can give of his best in isolation.

It cannot have helped Bennett that his friends failed to realise that he was essentially a composer for the piano, a composer of the range (not necessarily the stature) of Chopin; instead of recommending him to perfect what he could already do well, they advised him to try his hand at what he could not do at all. Thus Mendelssohn told the critic J W Davison, 'He ought to come out with some large work and say "Here I am, I am Bennett"'; while Schumann suggested that 'in order to give his fame the spur he should throw himself into grand works, a symphony, an opera.'

Persuaded against his better judgment, Bennett wasted the best part of two years on a stillborn project for chorus and orchestra called *Zion*. It should be added that though his works sound so fluent, composition did not come easily to him: he once said that he could only compare the production of a composition to the acutest form of bodily pain. Writing music in fact for Bennett was a source neither of income, nor public acclaim, nor personal relaxation: three formidable deterrents. A possible fourth and still more fundamental one — that he had run out of creative ideas — will be discussed at the appropriate point during the following description of his solo piano works.

Bennett wrote the first four of these before ceasing to be an Academy student. The *Capriccio* in D minor, opus 2, originally intended (I have no doubt) as the finale of the First Piano Concerto, is chiefly remarkable for the easy handling of sonata form which — either with or without development — was to prove Bennett's first choice for most of his larger piano solos. The *Six Studies in the form of Capriccios*, opus 11, mark a notable advance. Ostensibly they deal with various technical matters — No 1 is a study in double-thirds and crossed hands, No 2 in legato playing, No 3 in rapid triplets — but like the best of their kind their chief interest is musical. The first of the set to be composed was No 4 in F minor, a fiery study in repeated chords needing wrists of steel. Even more passionate is the final movement in G minor, which was Schumann's favourite, a hail of octaves with a masterly diminuendo in its closing bars. So much for Ernest Walker's notion that the chief characteristic of Bennett's style is a 'delicate, rather shy refinement'. (An orchestral version of this study was used as the finale of the early, unpublished Symphony in G minor.)

With the *Three Musical Sketches* (next in order of composition, despite the opus number 10) Bennett achieved one of the greatest successes of his career — so great, indeed, that these slight but charming pieces have entirely overshadowed the more important works that followed. Part of that success was certainly due to the composer's own interpretation of them; Schumann, who called the pieces themselves 'musical Claude Lorraines', described his playing of *The Fountain* as 'really magical in its effect'. In the first of the *Sketches*, Bennett needs only a few telling strokes to bring the calm, deep stillness of *The Lake* before us; the turbulent *Millstream*, equally unmistakable and effective, sounds conventional by comparison. *The Fountain*, however, is not the elaborate cascade you might expect, but witty, sparkling, even impudent.

I personally, however, would willingly exchange them all for the first of the *Three Impromptus*, opus 12, Bennett's next completed composition. Notice the placing of the second subject in the tenor register, a very characteristic Bennett texture. The other two movements are not quite on this high level; indeed the second, after a rather limp start in E major, only pulls itself together when it changes midway into the minor key. The last impromptu is a whirlwind affair of presto sextuplets, calling for an absolutely dazzling display of bravura execution. Beneath all the virtuosity, however, the structure is taut and firm.

During the next eight years, which I have designated Bennett's second period, he wrote the four works on which his reputation as a composer for solo piano must ultimately depend. First comes the Piano Sonata No. 1 in F minor, opus 13, dedicated to Mendelssohn. If I had to select one piece in order to demonstrate to a sceptic the validity of Schumann's claim that Bennett 'has a great deal of one kind of genius', the first movement of this sonata is the one I should choose. Previous works had already revealed Bennett's understanding of the instrument and grasp of design, though never on so large a scale as in this sonata. But the power and depth of musical thought are altogether new, and so are the sustained concentration and seriousness of purpose. This first movement is followed by an admirably concise and rousing scherzo, and a slow movement which begins with seemingly unpromising chords that flower out into a finely expressive lyrical continuation. (But the expressiveness is in the music: woe betide any pianist who attempts to add any on his own account.) Only the finale disappoints to some degree; was Bennett a little too hasty in his understandable anxiety to finish the work in time for a friend's wedding-day? There is a certain monotony induced by a lack of rhythmic and textural variety, and (in my view) the exactness of the recapitulation was a mistake. But the subdued ending, though difficult to bring off, is certainly very impressive.

No weakness of this kind mars the *Fantasia in A*, opus 16, dedicated to Schumann, to all intents and purposes a second sonata with no break between movements. Here the finale is as perfectly controlled in form as it is passionate in feeling, and it is crowned by a splendid outburst of

70

sustained lyricism. These are big words, but I see not the remotest prospect of being made to eat them. It is preceded by a pastoral (marked 'moderato con grazia'), a scherzo and a canzonetta which is little more than an interlude linking the second and the fourth movements. Only the elaborate formal scheme of repeats in the scherzo strikes me as unsatisfactory: were I editing the work for performance today I would recommend some omissions, reducing the scheme AABA—Trio—ABA codetta to the shorter one of ABA—Trio—A codetta.

Schumann hailed the *Three Romances*, opus 14, written between the Sonata and the *Fantasia*, as 'a great step in advance'. The first movement — a shade repetitious, perhaps — is richer in texture and bolder in harmony than hitherto; and if it is pervaded by a certain Schumannesque atmosphere, we are soon restored to a more familiar and comfortable lyricism in the second, which could easily be subtitled 'Song without Words'. Do not, however, underrate it; it is far and away Bennett's most successful essay in this style, and the main melody displays surprising strength of character when it modulates into the minor key. As for the finale, in which the conflicting demands of virtuosity and musical content are reconciled in a masterly fashion, it is (to borrow an exclamation of Mendelssohn's) 'Bennett, *all* Bennett'.

What do the official historians of British music have to say about the Sonata, the *Romances* and the *Fantasia*? The answer is: nothing. Eric Blom makes no mention of *any* of the solo piano works, Henry Davey shows familiarity with nothing later than the *Musical Sketches*; Ernest Walker, who reveals a great deal more understanding of, and sympathy with, Bennett than most, leaps straight from opus 10 (*the Sketches*) to opus 37; and even W H Hadow, Bennett's chief champion, reveals an almost total ignorance of Bennett's mature piano compositions when he writes, 'the essential qualities of his work are its transparence, its evenness, and its skill of draughtsmanship ... if we want vehemence and passion and glowing canvas we had better look elsewhere'. If the Sonata, the *Fantasia* and the finale of the *Romances* do not display vehemence and passion, I simply do not understand what the words can be supposed to mean.

Bennett followed these three masterpieces by a work which is in the nature of a relaxation — the *Three Diversions*, opus 17, for piano duet, which should be mentioned here if only for the fact that the first began life as a piano solo. They make a charming entertainment, perhaps lighter in character and more Mendelssohnian than usual, with a particularly sparkling finale. If no advance, this work is at least no retrogression. But immediately after come the first signs that Bennett was perhaps drying up; and it became legitimate to wonder whether, after six years of steady development, Bennett was at last beginning to run out of ideas, to 'repeat himself', to 'become involved in a mannerism'. The list of works which gave rise to these suspicions of Schumann (excluding the original cause of his disenchantment, the *Caprice* for piano and orchestra, opus 22) comprises an *Allegro Grazioso*, opus 18, a complacent piece that does nothing that the composer had not already done before and done better; two pieces without opus number, *Genevieve* and an *Album Leaf*, both sounding faded and old-fashioned yet curiously evocative, like flowers preserved by pressing between the leaves of an old book; *Rondo Piacevole*, opus 25, practically an anthology of Bennett's weaker points which may be explained, if not excused, as a first attempt to write a teaching piece for less advanced pupils; and *Two Characteristic Studies*, opus 29, also *déja vu*. These were completed around the end of the period under discussion — probably as a contribution to a collection of *Études de Perfectionnement* edited by Moscheles — but not published as a separate work until four years later.

One might, then, be justified in assuming that by 1837 Bennett was finished as a composer, had he not, in 1841, written the *Suite de Pièces*, opus 24, which drew from Schumann the comment that 'Bennett's works have continued to increase in originality', and which has some claim to be considered his greatest work for piano solo. In most of the six movements the composer tackles problems he never attempted before; where he covers old ground there are everywhere immense gains due to greater austerity of style and compression of thought. The opening toccata in C sharp minor, monothematic but tonally in sonata-form, is an excellent example of the latter. No 2 is a series of *andante* questions with *allegretto* answers, while No 4 is an unusual combination of chorale and arabesque. Both these two were singled out for special praise by Schumann. My own preference is for the fifth and sixth movements, the former a duple-time scherzo in F minor which begins *piano e staccato* and ends in flat-out hammering for both hands, the latter a finale displaying all Bennett's old energy but also a breadth not hitherto to be found in his music.

In Bennett's third period we are dealing no longer with a composer, but with a teacher who did a little writing in his spare time. Not surprisingly most of it is comparatively simple music, presumably intended for his pupils. In this category come the *Introduction and Pastorale, Rondino, and Capriccio*, opus 28, which — apart from the introduction which sounds as though it had strayed from *Hymns A. and M.* — is at any rate the *best* butter; a set of variations, opus 31, which come to a perfunctory and disappointing end as though the composer had suddenly lost interest in it; the *Minuetto Espressivo* of 1854 — like Elgar's salon music, so perfectly done that one can't help admiring it despite oneself — and the totally empty Rondeau *pas triste, pas gai*, opus 34, a piece sans sadness, sans gaiety, sans ideas, sans everything.

But the *Preludes and Lessons*, opus 33, a series of 30 miniatures employing all the customary major and minor key signatures once each, are quite another story. The *Preludes* are mostly little more than introductory flourishes, often in free recitative; but the *Lessons* are fairly extensive, being sometimes designed as characteristic pieces (a march or a minuet), sometimes as descriptive ones (*Zephyrus, The Butterfly, The Rivulet*), and sometimes as short studies affording practice in a particular technical problem, like trills or octaves. One little piece is an admirable two-part invention, and I only wish there had been more such contrapuntal essays in the set, for who could have written them better than the most prominent English Bach champion of his generation? With this one reservation, the *Preludes and Lessons* are quite brilliant, and it is no surprise to learn that, teaching pieces though they are, the composer often used to play a group of them at his concerts 'with telling effect'.

There remain the few works intended for the concert pianist alone, and these all have considerable merits. First comes the superb *Scherzo* (sometimes known as *Capriccio Scherzando*), opus 27. Like opus 2, this began life as part of a larger design; it was undoubtedly conceived as one of the movements of the Piano Trio in E minor which Bennett had planned to write as a companion-piece to the elegant Chamber Trio in A, opus 26. The *Toccata*, opus 38, employs a good deal of what Walker calls 'the rapid surface glitter ... for which a sort of immaculately neat emotionless precision is the main requisite', but then that is what a toccata is for. The two main themes provide unity in diversity, since both begin with fragments of a descending and/or ascending chromatic scale. Effective though the *Toccata* is, my own preference is for the *Rondeau à la Polonaise*, opus 37, because of the greater attractiveness of the thematic material. Lacking the stimulus of any further commissions (Bennett had been invited to write the *Toccata* by the Netherlands Society for the Encouragement of Music, and the *Rondeau à la Polonaise* by Messrs Payne of Leipzig) he wrote nothing more of importance until the very end of this third period. Then in 1856, as if sensing that this was his last chance to turn himself once again into a composer, he began a major series of piano pieces, one for each month of the year. He had completed the first two when in March he was elected to the Chair of Music at Cambridge, and the whole plan was brought to an abrupt end.

I must confess that I approached the surviving pieces, *January* and

February, with expectations of (at best) some further additions to Bennett's published salon music; but once again I proved the truth of Nero Wolfe's dictum that pessimists receive only pleasant surprises. The old mastery of technique is there all right, but there is a deeper seriousness of purpose without concessions to sentimentality, a greater richness and variety of texture, and many original touches in the overall design. Had this sequence of pieces been completed on the same high level, it would not only have ranked with the four masterpieces of his second period, but would also have demonstrated conclusively that Bennett was not diverted from his creative career by any lack of musical ideas. Both are large-scale pieces in a minor key and basically sombre in mood with, however, plenty of contrasting light and shade. A one-word description (mine, not the composer's) of *January* would perhaps be fantasia; of *February* (which is marked 'con moto, serioso'), a waltz.

Bennett was destined to rouse himself once again, during the fourth and final period of his life. After writing in 1863 and 1871 two little occasional pieces — a *Praeludium* for a favourite pupil and a Mozartian *Sonatina* (intended to be the first of a series) for his grandson, Bennett turned once again to the sonata and between 1869 and 1873 completed his opus 46, *The Maid of Orleans*.

Since Bennett was a cricket enthusiast, it may not be inappropriate to recall that even Bradman was dismissed for nought on his last Test appearance. Bennett's last innings was also a failure, though not quite total. He was undoubtedly greatly moved by Schiller's play *Joan of Arc*, but in the second and third movements he failed to translate his emotions into valid musical terms and the thematic material is insufficiently striking to sustain the design. More surprisingly, even Bennett's keyboard sense deserts him in the finale, no doubt grown rusty from disuse. How much more remarkable, then, by contrast with the rest, is the opening slow movement. This simple and touching pastoral is as beautiful as anything Bennett ever wrote:

Geoffrey Bush as a choirboy at Salisbury Cathedral.

[Handwritten letter]

this will all seem very prosy, or dd-foggy-ish
to you, I fear — but there is no short
cut.

I should not take the trouble to say
all this unless I felt you had imagination
& the desire to say something in music — so
you must not regard it as derogatory, or take
offence.

Let me hear if or when you are
likely to be in London, and if you will
give me plenty of notice I will arrange for
you to come & play some of your work to me, when
I may be able to help you ~~~~~~ more than
I can by letter. My London address is :-

The Studio
14th Gunter Grove
Chelsea, S.W. 10

Telephon, Flaxman, 0883.

So on with your composition, & do not hesitate
to ask my advice or opinion on anything you write
which you think good :

Yours sincerely
John Ireland

An invitation to Chelsea: part of John Ireland's first letter.

First page of the manuscript of
'Four Songs from Herrick's Hesperides' (1949).

Sterndale Bennett — portrait by Sir John Millais.

Sir Charles Stanford (reproduced by kind permission of the Director of the Royal College of Music).

Sir Hubert Parry (reproduced by kind permission of the Director of the Royal College of Music).

With conductor Nicholas Braithwaite at the Lyrita recording of Geoffrey Bush's Symphony No 1.

11. Two song-writers

Song-writing spanned the entire creative career of both Stanford and Parry. The earliest of the latter's songs to be printed appeared while he was still a schoolboy at Eton; his setting of *The sound of hidden music* (published posthumously) was finished on his last birthday. Stanford's opus I consisted of eight songs from George Eliot's *The Spanish Gypsy*; his *Songs of an Elfin Pedlar* were written only a few months before his death. Their contemporaries were united in admiring Stanford's Irish cycles and Parry's 12 sets of *English Lyrics*; but — in the case of Parry, at any rate — they were incapable of analysing the nature of their achievement. This was due not so much to lack of perception as ignorance of their own musical past. Purcell's light had already begun to shine in the darkness, thanks to the pioneering publications of the Purcell Society, but Parry's fellow musicians comprehended it not. The obituary tributes in Charles L Graves' biography of the composer, paid by R O Morris, J A Fuller Maitland and Harry Plunket Greene respectively, are a mine of misinformation: 'His melody ... follows both the sense and the accentuation of the words with a fidelity that no English writer before him had ever approached.' 'His wonderful skill in accentuation, or as it is sometimes called *declamation* ... is unrivalled among his countrymen.' 'Bach was about the only one who used [the melisma] pictorially until Parry adopted it as one of his means of expression.'

Such misconceptions, however wide of the mark, do at least spring from an appreciation of Parry's genius; whereas our generation seems unable even to recognise its existence. For today's casual critic Parry was a servile imitator of Brahms, ignorant of orchestration and concerned only with the production of a too-hastily-composed series of festival cantatas.

Leaving aside the fact that it is impossible to consider orchestration at all outside the context of the music being orchestrated, Parry's first love was for instrumental music. Though no public performer he was a fine pianist, and had studied instrumental technique with the most accomplished and adventurous English composer of his time, the expatriate H Hugo Pierson. The fruitful result of the latter's teaching can be found in such splendid scores as the *Symphonic Variations* and the *Overture to an Unwritten Tragedy*. And if in later years Parry devoted a disproportionate amount of time to supplying the wants of provincial choruses, circumstances rather than inclination were responsible. Unless a composer of Parry's generation could obtain a hearing for his works in Germany (Stanford was fortunate in this respect), his only public platform was the choral festival. While it is true that the pressure of administrative duties at the Royal College of Music, coupled with performance deadlines, did on occasion lead to work insufficiently considered and hastily written down, the exact opposite is the case with the music he wrote for his own pleasure and in his own time — the chamber music, the late organ works, and above all the songs.

The first step to a just appraisal is to recognise that Parry's songs do not exhibit qualities which can be severally identified and dissected in isolation. A few characteristics may be described in general terms: they are lyrical (though neither as simple or spontaneous as the best of Stanford's), they display an understanding of the human voice, they reject any striving after effect, and they avoid all mechanical repetition (a strophic song is a rarity in Parry's work). But their real strength is that they are indivisible wholes. Each song is conceived as a single entity to which every element in the design — vocal line, piano texture, motivic development, close attention to the meaning, atmosphere and accentuation of the text — make a significant contribution. Voice and piano, words and music, form a completely integrated partnership in a way that recalls the work not of Brahms but of Hugo Wolf. (This will come as no surprise to those who remember that the music of Wagner was one of Parry's first loves, and that in his youth he was an enthusiastic visitor to Bayreuth.)

A characteristic example of Parry's treatment of voice and piano can be found in the second set of *English Lyrics*: *Take, o take those lips away*. To begin with the singer is given the lead. At the words 'But my kisses bring again' an independant instrumental melody emerges in the pianist's right hand, which the composer employs in counterpoint with the vocal line to built up a passionate climax. As this subsides the voice remains suspended on an unresolved minor sixth, leaving the piano to complete the musical sentence with a simple but deeply satisfying cadence:

A more extended example of what may loosely be called Wagnerian methods is to be found in another work of the same period, the splendid *Four Sonnets by William Shakespeare*. Parry began by setting the sonnets in the German translation of Bodenstedt, perhaps under the influence of his teacher Pierson. He then completely rewrote the vocal line (while retaining the piano part intact) in accordance with the quite different demands of English prosody. The two versions were printed one above the other, providing a fascinating study in the art of declamation:

It is not surprising to find Shakespeare bringing out the best in Parry, for he had a special affinity with the classics of English poetry. When it was a question of contemporary literature, however, the 'impeccable taste' attributed to him by his biographer instantly vanished. His choice seemed to depend not so much on 'fastidious literary judgement' as on personal friendship; the man to whom he had the most frequent recourse, Julian Sturgis — mercilessly pilloried by Bernard Shaw for his 'fustian' libretto for Sullivan's *Ivanhoe* — was a fellow Etonian. For settings of contemporary poetry in the tradition of John Barnett's 'Lyric Illustrations' of *his* contemporaries Byron, Wordsworth and Shelley, we must go to Stanford. Browning, Tennyson, Bridges and Whitman inspired some of Stanford's best work; moreover, he collaborated with Tennyson in two of the latter's theatrical ventures*, and turned to Bridges for the text of his oratorio *Eden*. Early in his career Stanford also wrote two very attractive groups of songs to the original German of Heine. As the years went by, however, Stanford developed one weakness: he could not resist verses which expressed, in an embarrassing Anglo-Irish dialect, a sentimental nostalgia for the country of his birth. Life in Ireland seems to have had much the same fascination for him as life under the linden tree had for Mahler; both were to be enjoyed at a very safe distance.

Parry's twelve sets of *English Lyrics* are notable for their wide variety of mood and their astonishing consistency of craftsmanship. The latter was not the result of chance but (as can be seen from a study of the surviving manuscripts) of unremitting hard work. For two of the songs

* *Queen Mary* (Lyceum: 1876) and *Becket* (1892).

alone — *My heart is like a singing bird* and *Dream pedlary* — there survive a total of 13 pages of sketches and a further 19 pages of virtually complete drafts. (There is reason to suppose that this total is not complete, and in any case it does not include fair copies.) Parry took infinite pains to see that the finished work was the best he could do; he rewrote bars 40–43 of *Where shall the lover rest* at least four times, in order to improve the vocal line *and* the piano figuration *and* the harmonic structure. To make sure that revisions were correct, not merely in themselves but in context, Parry's habitual custom was to rework a song in its entirety, perhaps for the sake of only half-a-dozen bars. If there was a possibility of further improvement he was prepared to revise right up to the last moment. Before sending the copy of *Why so pale and wan, fond lover?* to the printer, Parry struck out the original piano part of bars 40–41:

and substituted a radically different version:

Other corrections might be made still later, at the proof stage — for example bars 43–46 of the piano part of *No longer mourn for me* and all of bars 50–52 of *A stray nymph of Dian*. Exceptionally — as in bar 35 of *When comes my Gwen* — a final decision might be deliberately postponed until the arrival of the proofs. (In the margin Parry instructed the printer to 'leave out for the present' the left-hand arpeggios, so that he could reconsider them at leisure.)

It is impossible to study these manuscripts without an increased respect for Parry's craftsmanship and a greater understanding of the art of musical composition. Such was the care bestowed on each individual phrase that Parry might well have anticipated Stravinsky's claim: 'I begin with technique and end with inspiration.' No detail was too small to receive attention. Consider how the accentuation of two adjectives in bar 12 of *Bright star* is subtly altered for the better:

or, in *Lay a garland on my hearse*, how an adequate piece of declamation is converted, by tiny modifications of melodic shape and rhythm, into a striking one:

It is equally fascinating to watch the emergence in three stages of a complete musical sentence (*Nightfall in winter*, bars 30–33; note that Parry originally conceived the song a semitone higher):

Not surprisingly, especial pains are taken over climaxes; in bars 23–25 of *There be none of Beauty's daughters* we can see a melodic phrase being extended upwards:

and in bars 46–47 of *Dirge in woods* another being extended downwards:

The merits of all these revisions are immediately obvious; in some ways it is even more instructive to study alterations whose purpose is by no means apparent at first sight. In the original vocal part of *To blossoms* there is an attractive anticipation of the beat on the word 'why' in bar 7; this has been made possible by restricting the duration of the previous word 'tree' to a crotchet:

tree, Why——— do ye fall

In the final version a minim has been allocated to 'tree' and the syncopation sacrificed:

tree, Why do ye fall

Why Parry should have preferred a duller piece of accentuation seems inexplicable — until one discovers, by practical experiment, that the average singer needs to snatch a breath before attacking the accented E flat.

Corrections are by no means confined to the voice part. As already indicated, the piano is an equal partner and receives equal attention, with results that will surprise no-one who is familiar with Parry's idiomatic keyboard writing in such works as the Second Piano Sonata. Sometimes a passage which is perfectly satisfactory in itself has to make way for the development of a motif which has been announced in the opening bars of a song; such a procedure (which makes a notable contribution to that unity which is the outstanding feature of Parry's best work) can be found in bar 21 of *Why so pale and wan* — another song which was originally conceived in a higher key:

The same song contains one surprising miscalculation — in bar 36 a heavy accent is placed on the absurdly insignificant syllable 'of'. It was much more characteristic of Stanford to ride roughshod over a poet's prosody if he felt that the musical conception demanded it. (At the final cadence of *his* setting of *Why so pale and wan* the strongest accent is allotted not to the word 'take' but to the relatively unimportant 'her'.) This, incidentally, was not Parry's first attempt to tackle Suckling's advice to fond lovers. A draft survives of a version which begins in triple time and changes to duple only for the final verse. Although Parry discarded this setting, it is — because more dramatic — arguably more successful.

Another incidental discovery to emerge from a study of the manuscripts is that Parry was a composer who liked his music performed one way one day and another another. As a result we are sometimes presented with equally effective but quite incompatible ways of performing the same passage. The closing vocal phrase of *Armida's garden* is a case in point:

A casual glance at Stanford's music for voice and piano, like a dip into the bran-tub at a fun-fair, may well prove unlucky — for like so many people to whom writing music comes as naturally as breathing, Stanford was a most uneven composer. But a more thorough investigation will reveal upward of 30 songs as fine as anything written by the more consistent Parry, and of a still greater variety. On the one hand are delicate miniatures written on the head of a pin, such as *To carnations* — a mere 13 bars long — or the children's song *Windy nights*; on the other are huge canvases like *Prospice* or *The battle of Pelusium*, in which shifting emotions are portrayed and long-range tonality handled with masterly authority. But though Stanford's inspiration may have been more fitful, his pursuit of technical perfection was as untiring as Parry's. This can be demonstrated, not from the manuscripts (most of which are missing), but from the extensive revisions undertaken by the composer when the second edition of a song was in prospect. These revisions took different forms: in *La belle Dame sans merci* Stanford confined himself to making numerous improvements in detail, whereas in *Sterne mit den goldnen Füsschen*, op. 4, no. 1, he rewrote virtually the whole of the second page. Particularly striking is the way in which the singer's final phrase was reshaped into an elegant arch of melody above an unchanged piano accompaniment:

Exactly the opposite is true of the first of the *Three songs*, op. 43, to poems by Robert Bridges. Here, Stanford recomposed the piano part while retaining the vocal line virtually unaltered. The result, incidentally, is rather curious; both versions of the song have distinct merits of their own, so that choosing between them is an almost impossible task.

Song-writing was decidedly Stanford's métier. There was no temptation to lapse into the academicism which all too often marred his instrumental compositions, but plenty of scope for the lyrical and dramatic talents which led Bernard Shaw* to proclaim him the rightful heir of Arthur Sullivan. GBS, who admired Stanford's settings of Browning's Cavalier poems as much as he detested 'impossible trash' like *The Revenge*, declared that 'with the right sort of book, and the right sort of opportunity in other respects, Stanford might produce a powerful and brilliant opera without creating any of the amazement which would certainly be caused by such a feat on the part of his academic rivals.' He also unerringly perceived that Parry (an agnostic) would never find his most fruitful source of inspiration in the Bible, but among the masterpieces of English verse: '*Judith* was a hard blow to bear from him ... I have hardly treated him with common civility since; but now that his genius, released from an unnatural and venal alliance, has flown back to the noble poetry that was its first love, let the hatchet be buried — and *Judith* with it as soon as possible.' Parry himself, who in a fit of self-reproach once threw the score of *Judith* out of the window, would surely have been the first to acknowledge Shaw's discernment.

---

* Bernard Shaw: *Music in London 1890–94*; I 227, II 308, I 93.

12. A footnote to Elgar's 'Enigma'

When Ian Parrott solved the problem of Elgar's 'Enigma' he must have had something of the same sense of satisfaction that Oedipus felt when he solved the riddle of the Sphinx — with the added bonus that no plague threatens the university town of Aberystwyth, where Dr Parrott has for many years been Professor of music*. He put forward his solution tentatively at first in his book on Elgar in the Master Musicians series (Dent, 1971), then definitively in the periodical *Music and Letters* (Jan. 1973). He reached his conclusions by the sublimely simple method of paying attention to *what Elgar actually said*; though, like all sublimely simple things, it first required someone to think of it. One rather tricky preliminary was needed: the problem, like Siamese twins, had to be operated on and split into its two quite separate constituent parts. The first of these (Elgar's choice of the word 'Enigma' and its implicit 'dark saying') was elucidated when Dr Parrott discovered that the composer must have heard the twelfth verse of I. Corinthians XIII read in the Latin of the *Vulgate* when he attended Mass on Quinquagesima Sunday. The second — of more widespread interest — was a specifically musical puzzle: what was the familiar theme that lay concealed beneath the orchestra's first 17 bars?

Previous would-be solvers had created an impassable barrier for themselves by making the unwarrantable assumption that this second theme *could be played in counterpoint* with the first. What Elgar actually said was that 'through and over the whole set another and larger theme "goes" but is not played — so the principal theme never appears, as in some late dramas [of Maeterlinck] the chief character is never on stage'. (Even if a melody had been discovered which fitted contrapuntally with Elgar's original, it could still not have gone 'through and over the whole set' for the good and sufficient reason that the structure of many of the variations does not follow that of the theme.)

The notion of counterpoint once disposed of, the way was open for an intuitive grasp of the correct solution. (I say 'intuitive', but it could equally well have been the end product of one of those series of diagrams beloved by undergraduate analysis students which reduce extended compositions to a handful of semibreves linked by dotted lines.) B flat, A, C, B natural — the name of Bach in musical notation — is one of the few

---

* He retired from the post in 1983.

motifs which Elgar might reasonably have expected to be known by all his listeners. Evidence of Elgar's own devotion to Bach is everywhere to be found, from his orchestration of the *Fantasia and Fugue* in C minor for organ to his reference in a Birmingham speech to 'the greatest musician that ever lived'.

Why did Elgar never reveal the solution to an expectant public? Because, like all true puzzle addicts, he knew that the only satisfaction to be had from a riddle is arriving unaided at the answer. (When at a pub session the composer Thea Musgrave was offered detailed directions for finding the Ladies in return for the solution of a particularly baffling problem which she had propounded, she declared that she could find the former for herself and that it was our business to discover the latter.) On one occasion, however, Elgar did offer a hint so very broad that it almost amounted to a give-away. The incident is described in Dora Powell's *Edward Elgar: memories of a variation* (OUP, 2nd edition, 1947). Mrs Powell was well aware of Elgar's musical preferences; elsewhere in the book she records his recommendation that 'you should begin the day by playing a Bach fugue'. This explains Elgar's retort when she pleaded ignorance in the hopes of prising the solution out of him: 'Well, I'm surprised. I thought that you, of all people, would guess it.'

This conversation occurred during a visit to the Elgars' house (the anagrammatic Craeg Lea) at Malvern during November 1899. Alice was ill in bed, and 'Dorabella' had been summoned to assist with the house, the invalid and the composer — the last of which duties involved helping Elgar to pack for a visit to Leeds. After a weekend largely spent in correcting the proofs of *Gerontius*, it was time to get ready to leave:

> Monday morning arrived and I thought the Lady much better. The packing was duly done and the clothes that E.E. was to change into were put ready. I ordered his cab. He was playing Bach fugues when I went in to say that everything was ready, and would he go and change?
>
> 'I'm not going: I'm going to stop at home.'
>
> I stood doubtfully by the door.
>
> 'Oh, very well; but you can bring my things in here, I'll change by the fire.'
>
> I brought them in and departed. The piano ceased for about three minutes and then began again, so, wondering what was happening, and getting anxious about the time, I ventured in. Bach was going on louder than ever and E.E. was sitting at the piano in a clean shirt, and trousers.
>
> 'You can just do some work and dress me. I'm not going to stop playing.'

Elgar's behaviour — so odd as to be inexplicable except as the sequel to Dorabella's questions about the 'Enigma' — should have come as a blinding revelation; but like the 'obvious' clues planted in her novels by Agatha Christie, it turned out instead to be blinding in the literal sense. Neither Mrs Powell nor (to the best of my knowledge) any of her readers ever succeeded in guessing the musical word which Elgar was acting out for her benefit in this characteristically zany charade.

13. Vaughan Williams and the stage

The appearance (in 1979) of a new recording of VW's ravishing Cotswold fairy-story *Hugh the Drover* gives rise to the melancholy reflection: why are the stage works of a born man of the theatre so neglected?

This seemingly simple question raises two others which demand to be answered first. Neglected by whom? Not by students and amateurs. Immediately after the death of an outstanding creative artist, his reputation usually undergoes a temporary decline; but in the annual list of performances issued by the National Federation of Music Societies, even during this period Ralph Vaughan Williams' name led all the rest. It is the professionals (one is sorely tempted to add *as always*) who are at fault. To take only one example: where was the English National Opera Company at the time of the 300th anniversary of the publication of Bunyan's *The Pilgrim's Progress*? Why was there no production of VW's opera at the Coliseum?

Secondly, by what right can Vaughan Williams be called a born man of the theatre? If one talks to Ursula Vaughan Williams, one soon learns that the stage was one of VW's chief preoccupations throughout his life. His teacher Stanford divined that this was his true métier, and urged him to go to Italy and soak himself in the opera performances at La Scala. (As usual in his dealings with Stanford, VW did the exact opposite, going to study in Germany with Max Bruch. As he confessed in later years 'I made the great mistake of trying to fight my teacher.' This did not of course prevent the emergence of his genius, but it may well have delayed it.) If evidence is required from the works themselves, what could be more theatrical (in the best sense) than *Job*? Consider the masterly way in which the characters of this 'Masque for Dancing' are depicted in music: Job himself, all patient tranquility, the three oily Comforters, and Satan — virile and athletic*, yet at the same time the epitome of evil. When an undergraduate I saw Helpmann interpret the latter rôle; the terrifying moment when Satan usurps God's throne made an unforgettable impression on me, surpassed only by his expulsion at the hands of the Sons of the Morning and his (literally) headlong fall from heaven.

---

* VW advised Anton Dolin, the first Satan, that Blake had intended him to be 'a *very* handsome man.'

Which brings us back to where we started: why do our professional opera companies ignore Vaughan Williams? It can hardly be lack of popular support. Between the wars, when *Hugh the Drover* did make regular appearances in the Sadlers Wells repertoire, it always commanded a large and enthusiastic audience. Hardly more convincing is the excuse that — to borrow an accusation made by the plaintiff in a recent divorce case — VW was 'in the habit of making unreasonable demands in the cinema' (for cinema read opera house). If ever there was a composer whose choice of subject matter and performance requirements were so exceptional as to verge on the eccentric (consider *The Cunning Little Vixen* and *The Makropoulos Case*, or, in the concert hall, the 11 extra trumpets needed for the *Sinfonietta*) it was surely Janáček; but this has not prevented the English National company from mounting the complete cycle of Janáček's operas, or the Welsh and Scottish National companies jointly from following suit. (As a fanatical admirer of the Czech composer I have less than no objection to this — only to its being done at VW's expense.) Neither merit nor chance are solely responsible for this situation; as so often in British musical affairs, we are at the mercy of anyone who finds himself in a position of authority. The vogue for Janáček is the result of the advocacy of the man who was until recently Musical Director at the Coliseum, Sir Charles Mackerras; just as the vogue for Nielsen is due to Robert Simpson and the vogue for Boulez to Pierre Boulez.

Of all Vaughan Williams' stage works only *The Pilgrim's Progress* can be described as unusually demanding; and that because (as Cambridge audiences discovered during the moving revival there in 1954) it is more of a spiritual experience than an opera. But nobody has ever seriously objected to *Parsifal* on that account. (Incidentally, this spiritual element — and the splendid use of the hymn-tune 'York' at the climax — would surely have met with the approval of Charles Ives.) *Riders to the Sea*, like all one-act operas, needs careful programming. There would have been no problem at all had VW carried out his intention of setting Synge's comedy *The Tinker's Wedding* as a companion piece; but since *Hugh the Drover* is on the short side, this will do almost equally well.

Ursula Vaughan Williams considers that her husband's operas have been slow to gain recognition because they generally got off to an appalling start. Certainly the British National Opera Company's première of *Hugh the Drover* in 1924 was only 'saved from disaster every few bars' by the alertness of the conductor, Malcolm Sargent, who 'pulled the chestnuts out of the fire in a miraculous way' — and by volunteer choral reinforcements from the Royal College of Music, where a series of private performances had preceded BNOC's official first night. The original producer of *The Pilgrim's Progress* entirely ignored the composer's explicit instructions for staging the fight with Apollyon as a shadow play, on the lines of Peer Gynt's struggle with the Boyg in the Richardson-Thorndyke production of Ibsen's poetic drama at the Old Vic; 'tepid' would seem to be the kindest adjective that can be applied to both performance and reception. On the other hand, many operas (*La Traviata, Gloriana*) have survived disastrous first nights; and my own recollection of the professional première of *Sir John in Love* in 1946, as a member of the audience, was that it was a most happy occasion.

Which brings us to the librettos. No fault can be found with those compiled by the composer himself from Bunyan and Shakespeare; *Sir John in Love* lays itself open to criticism solely by its temerity in challenging Verdi and Boito. (Perversely, VW professed to consider Nicolai a greater rival than Verdi — possibly this was a subconscious extension of his original feud with Stanford.) VW had been drawn to *The Merry Wives of Windsor* as a suitable subject for an opera ever since he had been responsible for the incidental music for this and other Shakespeare plays during Frank Benson's 1912 – 13 seasons at Stratford; he firmly believed that there should be at least one such opera written by one of Shakespeare's fellow-countrymen. The great strength of VW's libretto is his conception of the characters as real people. To quote Ursula: 'You can meet Mistress Quickly here in Camden Town any day of the week.' (It was this same realisation of the 'essential humanity' of Shakespeare's comic characters which made Terry Hands' Stratford production the most unexpected revelation of the present writer's theatre-going life.)

The librettos produced by other hands were not so successful. In particular, that of the operetta *The Poisoned Kiss* came in for such widespread criticism that Ursula Vaughan Williams has since given Evelyn Sharp's original text a thorough spring-cleaning. But in my view the libretto of *Hugh the Drover* has been unjustly maligned. Some of the language may be tiresome, but the plot (much of it, notably the prize-fight, originating with the composer) and the dramatic timing are excellent. These are the things that really matter in an opera libretto; consider how the taut structure of *Peter Grimes* makes up for any number of verbal infelicities. Harold Child, author of the text of *Hugh the Drover*, was recommended to VW by the then editor of the *Times Literary Supplement*; unfortunately his view of country people — that they were there to be laughed at — was quite contrary to Vaughan Williams' own conception of their humanity and natural dignity. However, as we can see from the composer's letters*, which have been reprinted in Ursula's biography, VW took infinite pains to get this and other matters put right. Moreover, Harold Child performed one service beyond price: he wrote lyrics which inspired VW to pour out an unending stream of melody of a quality which reduces at least one listening composer to ecstatic delight and envious despair in about equal proportions. 'By the way', Vaughan Williams wrote to Harold Child in August 1911, 'I am finding your words splendid to set.' No librettist could ask for a better testimonial.

It is a thousand pities that he never joined forces with Ursula to write a full-scale opera. One (based on two traditional ballads) was planned, but VW died before it could advance beyond the preliminary stages. Their only surviving operatic collaboration is Lord Lechery's song, which — like the Watchman's scene — was added to *The Pilgrim's Progress* at the thirteenth hour. This had a narrow escape: when Ursula appeared with the requested new text, she discovered that the composer had in the meantime produced a version of his own. Ursula was *not* best pleased — until both poems having been submitted anonymously to Steuart Wilson for his adjudication, the umpire decided in her favour.

After examining all these possible reasons for the neglect of Vaughan Williams' operas, one is forced, finally, to blame the indifference of the composer's countrymen. It is an old, old story. 250 years ago Roger North wrote (of the missing score of Purcell's *King Arthur*) 'there was so much admirable musick in that opera, that no wonder it's lost: for the English have no care for what's good, and therefore deserve it not.' In 1841 Michael Balfe, whose *The Bohemian Girl* was to go round the world, saw his plans for a national opera with a repertory of works by British composers sabotaged in spite of royal support. Stanford — a naturally-gifted opera composer if ever there was one — suffered even more than his famous pupil. Eric Walter White tells us that his *The Veiled Prophet* met with instantaneous success in Hanover but 'took twelve years to reach Covent Garden, and then only for a single performance in an Italian translation.' Only Benjamin Britten, by restricting the number of performers in his own company to the economically practicable, managed for a time to beat the system; but after his death the English Opera Group rapidly faded away.

An opera composer in this country lacks not only encouragement but the opportunity to learn his trade by practical experience in the theatre; Tippett did not see his first opera, *The Midsummer Marriage*, staged until he was 50 years old. Commissions are rare; and unless a composer is

---

* As always, VW filed the librettist's replies in his favourite storage-system, the wastepaper basket.

writing for a specific occasion he can only guess at the probable size of the orchestral pit and the best compass of his soloists. *Job* is a case in point; due to delays and difficulties in securing a stage performance, Vaughan Williams felt obliged to score it as a concert piece, using (for him) an exceptionally large orchestra. Consequently it later had to be scaled down for theatre band by Constant Lambert.

To return to the new recording of *Hugh the Drover*: will it give the opera a new lease of life on the stage — where it belongs? Ursula Vaughan Williams, contemplating the three cats who allow her to live in her house and the seventeen composers with whom she has collaborated, is very hopeful. (Seventeenth in line, appropriately enough, was recently composer-in-residence at VW's old school, Charterhouse.) Considered on merit, there could be no doubt about the opera; I have seen it work in the theatre and given any sort of chance it can work there again. To ensure its return to the stage, however, it is necessary to persuade those who control our musical destinies that an English National Opera depends not just on native performers singing in English but on a repertory built around the best operas written by British composers.

14. When I was young and twenty, I heard a wise man say ...

All musicians are familiar with the Purcell Society, the Vaughan Williams Trust and the headquarters of the Mechanical Copyright Protection Society, Elgar House. But how many have ever heard of Balfour's Wood or Gardiner Forest?

You can find their whereabouts in the top left-hand corner of Ordnance Survey Sheet No 179; and they commemorate not the music of Balfour Gardiner but the forestry work which he undertook from about 1925 onwards near his home in Dorset. For one of the most remarkable things about this very remarkable man was that in mid-career he suddenly abandoned composing in favour of agriculture; not from economic pressure (for he was a rich man), nor under the compulsion of some physical or mental decline (such as forced the premature retirement of Duparc, and to some extent that of Rossini), but as the result of personal decision, freely and deliberately arrived at.

According to Delius, Balfour had a theory that at a certain age a man ceases to be musical, and that he himself had already reached that age. ('Would that many others thought the same' was Delius's comment to Eric Fenby.) Another reason, this time advanced by Sir Thomas Armstrong, was that after Balfour came back from the 1914 war, he felt there was no place for the kind of music he liked and felt able to write. He was certainly discouraged, perhaps even embittered, by the fact that whereas the public greeted several of his lighter pieces with what seemed to him excessive enthusiasm, they took not the slightest interest in the major works into which he had put his heart. (To this day you will find a hundred people who can hum the theme of *Shepherd Fennel's Dance* to every one who has heard — even once — Balfour Gardiner's Symphony in D.)

All the same, Balfour did not entirely cut himself off from music and musicians — he gave much time and trouble to editing Delius's scores for the press, a service which is usually credited exclusively to Beecham — and towards the end of his life his interest in his own compositions was rekindled by performances organized or given by his friends. (He was particularly moved on one occasion by the singing of the Oxford Bach Choir in one of his choral works.) He was also, I think, touched by the affection and admiration of the undergraduate musicians he used to meet at Oxford during his periodic absences from his Dorset estate. He would entertain us about once a term with a rich Dorset goose, and even richer anecdotes about his life at Frankfurt, where he studied composition under Knorr. We repaid him in the only way in which the young can repay the old — by treating him as if he were exactly the same age as ourselves. I think he enjoyed our undergraduate impertinences, especially in artistic matters; I recall his half-horrified delight as we dragged him off to the Scala Cinema to see Shakespeare put through it in *The Boys from Syracuse*, or to the nearest gramophone-shop to hear *Largo al factotum* sent up by my favourite pin-up of that time, Judy Garland.

For Balfour himself was always a great slaughterer of sacred cows. He had no patience with people who sat respectfully through performances of the Bach unaccompanied violin sonatas, for he believed (as I do) that there is no noise quite so foul — no, not even the Concord's sonic boom — as that made by a violinist scraping backwards and forwards over three or four strings at once. Another of his targets was the folksong movement; he professed to believe that the metrical complexities of most folk melodies (by which their collectors set such store) were originally nonexistent, but had come into being because the singers from whose dictation they were notated were unable (owing to either the weaknesses of age or the strength of alcohol, or both) to exercise proper breath-control.

Musical asceticism he could not abide. I remember his appalled description of the first performance of a composition by X — or it may have been Y. 'There they were, the orchestral players, row on row of them, triple woodwind, horns, brass, strings, harps and percussion, as far as the eye could reach. And what did the composer do? He began with a solo viola. ...'

Balfour was agreeably illiberal in his utterances, but in no way did he allow his opinions to interfere with his generosities to other musicians. The celebrated series of concerts of British music which he gave in 1912 and 1913 contained works written by composers of widely differing musical persuasions; and, later on, the fact that he was temperamentally more sympathetic to the music of Delius than that of Holst did not make his treatment of the latter any less munificent. (When all Delius's money had been spent on unavailing attempts to stop the onset of paralysis, Balfour bought from him his house at Grez-sur-Loing and then gave it back to Delius to live in for his lifetime rent free; when Holst was due to go to Salonika in 1918, Balfour hired the Queen's Hall, the LSO and (Sir) Adrian Boult so that before he left the composer could hear the score of *The Planets* come alive in sound for the first time.)

And if Balfour was critical of other composers, he was even more trenchant about himself. 'I was a rotten composer,' he told me once. I think he had been listening to a broadcast of his *Comedy Overture*. 'Why they go on doing that old thing, I don't know.' He felt himself greatly deficient in technique compared with other composers, for instance his friend Frederic Austin, whom he always admired for his ability to find several solutions for each and every problem which confronted him in the course of a composition. At the same time he often found the academic technique which he *had* acquired at Frankfurt more of a hindrance than a help; so rigidly had conventional musical proprieties been drilled into him that once he found himself literally unable to put down on paper the unorthodox and disordant progression which he felt his conception demanded at that particular point. He was a connoisseur of orchestration, and had an unusual method of assessing the quality (or otherwise) of his own efforts. 'I go straight to the cello part,' he explained, 'and if it is all above middle C I know the piece is well scored.' In this as in other ways he was completely objective about his own works, as if the Balfour Gardiner who had written them was in some strange way a quite different person from himself. If — rarely — he felt they deserved praise, he gave it, thankfully. 'I listened to that old choral piece of mine the other day,' he said on another occasion, beaming all over his face. (I can't swear to it, but I am almost sure it was his setting of Masefield's *News from Whydah*.) 'And, do you know — it was *good*!'

I wish — for I am a fanatical admirer of *News from Whydah* — that I had had the presence of mind to borrow Fred Astaire's retort from the film *Second Chorus*, after his performance of the Gopak in Russian costume at a fifth-rate restaurant cabaret had been patronizingly praised by a customer in broken English: 'vos good.'

'Vos good?' snarled Astaire. 'Vos *good*? Vos *pairfect!*'

15. John Ireland: a personal impression

I. The man

That autumn a new assistant chaplain arrived at the school. This event, commonplace in itself — in those days chaplains appeared and disappeared almost unnoticed — gained great significance from the fact that this particular priest came from Chelsea, home of none other than John Ireland the composer. When he discovered that my heart was in the composing of sonatas rather than Latin proses, he promptly wrote to his famous parishioner about me. The reply was astonishing: 'Send me everything that boy has written'.

Little did John Ireland know what he was bargaining for. Nowadays I often spend hours sniffing cautiously round a single bar, like a dog encountering a suspicious lamppost; but then I used to pour the stuff on paper with reckless abandon, disregarding every consideration except that of adding one more to a Bradman-like total of opus numbers. Even ruthless pruning could not prevent the parcel being a formidable one. There followed (not surprisingly) several weeks' delay: then at last a letter in a strange handwriting (which later I got to know so well), postmarked Chelsea.

I searched in vain for any sentence that could remotely be construed as 'Hats off, gentlemen, a genius'. Instead, there was a great deal of kindly but sober advice:

> 'I see you are at present much in love with what I must call, for want of a better word, dissonance — the kind of dissonance, I mean, which has been in vogue mainly during the last 10 or 15 years. This is an extremely difficult medium to handle in a convincing way, and to do so (if one admits the works of Schönberg and Bartók and Hindemith to be convincing) implies, at any rate as a basis, a thorough and efficient working knowledge of harmony and counterpoint in the accepted sense. All the composers I have mentioned (and of course one could add Stravinsky) have undoubtedly been through a protracted and severe course of this kind of training before blossoming out into what may at first sight appear to be without rhyme or reason'.

After recommending a study of classical styles and strict counterpoint as a preliminary to 'sailing the uncharted seas which I see appeal so strongly to you just now', he added the warning 'but all this involves time and labour, and, in fact, musical composition is a whole-time job. This will all sound very prosy and old-fogey-ish to you, I fear, but then there is no short cut'. (Hard work and old-fogeydom are two themes which are constantly recapitulated in later letters: 'When I was your age I was considered a dangerous innovator — now you know what they think of me — a bloody old fogey. What does it matter? You should write to please yourself. But don't be too easily pleased'.)

Came the holidays — and with them an invitation to visit him at his Chelsea studio. Everything about the first visit was exciting — the trip on the No 11 bus to that romantically named fare-stage The World's End; the vast studio seemingly empty save for a grand-piano and a fiercely-burning stove, and John Ireland himself, to uninformed eyes a prosaic and even insignificant-looking person, but to me the composer of the Piano Concerto and of two pieces rather more within my limited pianistic reach (*The Darkened Valley* and *The Holy Boy*) and therefore the greatest man I had met or was ever likely to meet.

I returned home in a daze: such a daze, in fact, that I took the wrong train at Victoria and landed myself in some benighted suburb which neither I nor anyone I asked had ever heard of. Which somehow made the day even more magical than ever.

A visit to John Ireland became a regular feature of the school holiday after that, and I never lost the thrill of it. I would bring him my latest composition, and he would turn the manuscript over in an abstracted sort of way, before eventually opening it somewhere in the middle. Invariably he chanced on the very page where there was some weak passage or other which had gone in at that point because I had been unable to think of anything better. I never understood how, even before he spoke, he was able to make me realise my shortcomings, until I came across the phrase (in Thomas Mann's *Doctor Faustus*) 'the teacher is the personified conscience of the pupil'. Passages which seemed tolerable when looked at through my eyes immediately became intolerable when looked at through his — because in my heart of hearts I had really known they were intolerable from the word go.

John Ireland never gave me any formal instruction, but the help I received from these unofficial sessions was incalculable. He was always friendly, extremely patient, often encouraging and invariably critical. One page once made him declare that the very sight of it made him need seven beers. In his outspoken denunciation of anything he disliked he followed the example of his own teacher, Stanford, whose toughness he found as valuable as it was disagreeable. 'Vaughan Williams, Holst and myself', he once wrote to me, 'owe much to that great man, Stanford'.

Meanwhile at school I was being coached for a classical scholarship, and there seemed little prospect of my ever becoming a professional musician. Then, one day, John Ireland told me that he had heard of a composition scholarship being offered at Balliol, which he thought was just up my street. (He had in fact heard of it from one of his own pupils, who in Ireland's opinion was more of an organist than a composer: the accuracy of his assessment was borne out by the fact that as soon as the examiners heard his pupil play they offered him the organ scholarship on the spot.) Winning this composition scholarship, besides saving me from almost certain failure in the classical one, was the turning point in my life; from this time onwards — although the college made me continue with Latin and Greek — music was officially recognised as my main interest.

About this time I wrote a clarinet *Rhapsody* which was an improvement on my previous efforts, and John Ireland came up to Oxford for the first performance. The players and I took him for dinner to the George, and I think he thoroughly enjoyed being made a fuss of by the younger generation. Possibly this is why he retained a strong affection for this *Rhapsody*. Later on he tried to interest a London publisher in it, and took up the cudgels on my behalf when the BBC wrote to inform me that their reading panel considered it unsuitable for broadcasting. Unfortunately for the BBC, John Ireland was at this time chairman of their reading panel, and was therefore in a position to know that he and his colleagues had, in fact, unanimously recommended it. On hearing that I had been told the opposite, Ireland lodged an immediate and furious protest, an act requiring more courage than the layman might realise; since the BBC is the composers' chief, indeed perhaps only, employer nowadays, it takes a bit of nerve to risk antagonising those in charge of it. I never received any apology or explanation; but I got the broadcast.

Years later I asked him if I might show my thanks for all he had done for me by dedicating a piece of mine to him. He expressed a preference for the *Rhapsody*, but since this was already occupied, so to speak, by the clarinettist for whom I had written it, I proposed my new Violin Sonata, which I proceeded to play through to him for his approval. After listening in silence for about a quarter-of-an-hour, he suddenly interrupted:

'This is rather long for a first movement, isn't it?'

'There is only one movement'.

(Short pause).

'Good'.

Before the war John Ireland was for many years organist of St Luke's, Chelsea, and when the post fell vacant again after the war he recommended me for the job. I wasn't much of a success. The war had decimated the considerable musical establishment, and besides a handful of untrained boys, only a tenor aged 68 and a bass aged 86 remained. More alarming — to an organist like myself, who needs constant reassurance that all is well before proceeding from one note to the next — was the timelag caused by siting the organ console and its elaborate pipe-cum-electronic apparatus at opposite ends of the church. Moreover, the Vicar tended to base his musical opinions on the reaction of the congregation, and he placed particular reliance on one whose authority he considered unimpeachable for the curious reason that he was an Admiral.

My year there was chiefly memorable in that it enabled me to see quite a lot of John Ireland at a time when he was composing the *Satyricon Overture* and the music to the film *The Overlanders*. Both these works gave him a lot of trouble, the latter owing to the producer, who knew nothing of musical technique but had a very decided idea of what he wanted written. I remember at one recording session he complained that the music Ireland had composed for the taming of the wild horses, a wonderful jagged clarinet solo accompanied by pizzicato lower strings, sounded like a Sunday afternoon chamber concert. Only the ingenuity of the musical director, who devised a countermelody prominent enough to deceive the producer but not so prominent as to obscure Ireland's original conception, saved the situation.

As early as 1943 Ireland had thought of writing a choral work based on the *Satyricon*, a novel written during the reign of Nero by the Latin author Petronius, which attracted him by reason of 'its general atmosphere of roguery and vagabondage'. He was hindered by the fact that some of the text was at that time untranslated and considered untranslateable (though nowadays it would hardly cause the raising of an eyebrow). In 1944 the receipt of a commission for a purely orchestral work in honour of Sir Henry Wood's Jubilee Season at the Proms caused him to change his mind. He composed the opening of the overture there and then, but was forced by shortage of time to abandon it. In 1946 he resumed work, again for the Proms and again at short notice ('I was a fool to undertake it in the time available'); but on this occasion he carried it through successfully, though not without some misgivings about some unusual elements in the structure: 'I have got it sketched out, but would like six months to think about it. For one thing, I have made an experiment in the form, and am not yet sure if it is satisfactory. I have not made any recapitulation of the 1st subject until the Coda —

so the form stands:

    A. 1st subject, etc.
    B. 2nd subj., etc.
    C. Development section which contains a new theme.

This joins up to the section of A which leads to the 2nd subject (B) then the Coda, which is short, and based on the 1st subj., (A). It is an unusual way of treating the form. And the main sequence of keys is also unusual — not taking account of intermediate and modulatory passages the key centres are: A. E flat. G. C. D flat. F. and back to A for the Coda.'

Lack of time to think things over always bothered Ireland — in fact he altogether hated working at pressure to meet a deadline. During the war he composed incidental music for a BBC production of *Julius Caesar*, using the 'nice clear-cut sound' of eight wind, eleven brass, percussion and three doublebasses. For this task he was allowed a fortnight, which meant that he 'had to put everything else on one side and just stick at it all day every day and a good part of the night as well'. In my innocence I had written to him that I had enjoyed a holiday writing music, and he replied 'Well, well. Compared with writing the music for *Julius Caesar*, penal servitude would have been a recreation.'

Ireland's letters were always forthright, and never more so than when he was discussing his fellow-musicians. He could be generous, but compliments had to be earned. No living composer (not even himself) had, in his opinion, the right to the adjective 'great', with the possible exception of Sibelius; for him few, if any, modern works could stand comparison with Debussy's 'ravishingly beautiful and satisfying pieces' *Nuages* and *Fêtes*. But he admired Vaughan Williams's 5th Symphony (though that composer's music was largely antipathetic to him) for its 'sincerity and reticence', and he expressed great enthusiasm for the virtuosity of Britten's *The Turn of the Screw* and for the austerity of Alan Bush's Symphony No 1 in C major. He described the latter as 'very original, virile and well-made — clearly a work of considerable importance, written with no regard to the mob, the box-office or the publisher', and added 'I am anxious to hear it again.'

He listened carefully and critically to performances of his own work; he spoke unprintable things about one conductor who took his *London Overture* so fast that it was listed in the returns of the Performing Right Society not as a complete performance but as a 'short selection'. The best performance he ever heard of *Mai Dun* was given, so he told me, by Rudolf Schwarz: this at a time when that fine conductor was a favourite victim of London's hatchet-men.

104

He was always stimulating to talk to, and though he was famous for his pessimism, a touch of wry humour could be discerned even in his most pessimistic utterances. The last time I saw him, in the converted windmill facing Chanctonbury Ring to which he had moved after leaving Chelsea, we were discussing the changes of fashion which had led the BBC — for the first time I could remember — to discard his music from the Proms. (He didn't live long enough to hear it restored the following year: an episode wholly characteristic of English musical history). I comforted him with the assurance that the pendulum was bound to swing back again, adding that in artistic matters there were inevitably some ups and downs. 'Yes', he replied darkly, 'but more downs'.

II. The musician

The outbreak of war brought my regular visits to John Ireland to an untimely end. But there was compensation in the form of a series of letters written to me, first from Banbury and later from the little Essex village where Ireland had taken refuge with friends after escaping from the Channel Islands a few hours before they were invaded by the Germans. In the course of our correspondence a dispute arose over neo-classicism. Despite his admiration for Stravinsky's early works, Ireland had not cared for the Symphony in C, which he had heard on the radio in 1943, and feared (correctly) that I was longing to jump on that particular band-wagon. 'Don't you think that you should avoid that method, if you can think of any other? It is so easy to write in the style of Bach or Mozart or Gluck or Handel, sprinkled with a few wrong notes and some jazzy rhythmic perversions.' Being an opinionated young man of twenty-odd, I objected that the methods of many another great composer could be reduced to absurdity in this way; to which he replied 'Delius had a style of his own, and so has Vaughan Williams — though both are easy to imitate, as you point out. I note that (out of politeness — double question-mark) you have refrained from giving the simple recipe for *my* formula — if it is a formula — I am not aware that it is.'

I never replied to this at the time; but now, as an opinionated man of fifty-odd, I feel like having a try. Before starting, however, the point should be made that Ireland's musical preoccupations were not solely creative. Like practically every composer one can think of, Ireland in his time played many parts. He was a notable organist, choirmaster, composition teacher and pianist; in fact, when he came south on his fourteenth birthday to study at the Royal College of Music, he was enrolled as a piano pupil. (It wasn't long before he conceived a passionate ambition to study composition with Stanford; this ambition was realised when Parry heard a student performance of his First String Quartet and awarded him a scholarship on the spot.) His first professional job was as assistant organist and choirmaster at Holy Trinity, Sloane Street, for which he was chosen by Walter Alcock from a long list of more experienced applicants, although he was only 17 years old.* Nearly 30 years' service followed in various organ lofts, principally that of St Luke's, Chelsea — a vast, neo-Gothic pile just behind the old theatre in the King's Road. He appeared regularly as pianist in public performances of his own compositions, though he didn't have as much time to play the instrument as he would have wished. (He used to say that he practised either too little or — when a concert was approaching — too much.)

One of the occupations which reduced the amount of time available was teaching at his old college. His most notable achievement there was taking up the cudgels on behalf of a young scholarship candidate from Suffolk who for some unknown reason — possibly he was *too* brilliant — had aroused the antagonism of the other examiners. Ireland dealt with the situation in characteristic fashion: 'Either the boy is awarded a scholarship or I resign.' The boy in question was, of course, Benjamin Britten; and at the request of Frank Bridge, to whom he had already been going for lessons during the school holidays, he was enrolled as Ireland's composition student. Britten felt frustrated at the college because there were so few opportunities for trying out his compositions in performance; but during his time with Ireland he wrote several works of astonishing promise, including the String Quartet in D of 1931 and the choral variations *A Boy Was Born*.

To return to John Ireland's challenge; obviously there is no question here of giving a formula or recipe, let alone a simple one. Ireland was a complex musical personality and, as I hope to show, his character was formed by many different interests and influences. Merely to catalogue a handful of mannerisms would be as misleading as it would be superficial. Most composers tend to respond to an emotional situation which they have met before with the sort of music they have written before; and there are some turns of phrase, some harmonic progressions, some keyboard textures of which Ireland was particularly fond. In actual fact

---

* Ireland liked to recall that his youthfulness proved his undoing on one occasion; at choir practice he was too inexperienced to prevent the boys marching round and round the church bawling the principal motif of Stanford in B flat to the words of a popular song of the day: 'Army duff, army duff.'

there are not all that many of these recurring fingerprints, nor are they of any great importance. What *does* distinguish Ireland's music from that of his contemporaries is his entirely personal reaction to the problem which faced all of them at that particular moment in our musical history: how to recover a sense of identity in a country that had forgotten that such a thing as an English musical tradition had ever existed.

John Ireland was born into a century which had been dominated first of all by Mendelssohn and then by Brahms. It is easy to understand the reasons for this. As Nicholas Temperley has pointed out, the German style 'was central to European music at the time'; moreover, Germany was the only place where English composers could get a hearing. It was in Leipzig that Sterndale Bennett received an ovation for his Third Piano Concerto, in Hamburg that Hugo Pierson made his reputation with his music for the second part of Goethe's *Faust*, in Hanover that Stanford's first opera, *The Veiled Prophet*, was staged, and at Düsseldorf that *The Dream of Gerontius* was rehabilitated after the Birmingham fiasco. It is not surprising that John Ireland arrived in his teens at the Royal College of Music so thoroughly Germanised that Stanford declared his compositions to be 'all Brahms and water' and made him write music in the style of Palestrina for the whole of his first year. The spirit of Brahms had not been completely exorcised by the time Ireland came to write the Sextet for clarinet, horn and string quartet in 1898. The first three movements are technically faultless and in their conventional way delightful to listen to; the finale, however, marks a milestone in Ireland's development, for in it we can hear for the first time intimations of the composer's own authentic voice. Stanford strongly disapproved of this movement, and in one sense he was right. Since it was Ireland's first exploratory step into a new world, it was a clumsy, hesitating step. In another sense he was quite wrong — indeed, there could be no better illustration of Hans Keller's thesis that the successes of a student composer ought to be blue-pencilled, whereas the failures (because these alone are his own unaided work) should be encouraged.

For Holst and Vaughan Williams the path to freedom from German musical domination lay through folksong. Ireland felt not the slightest inclination to follow their example, though he did acknowledge the immense importance of the rediscovery of our heritage of Tudor choral music. The *chief* liberating factor, however, was the discovery that Germany did not have the monopoly of the mainstream of European music. Two other countries had things of equal importance to contribute and to which he could instantly respond. The first of these was Russia. Ireland heard the first performance in this country of Tschaikowsky's

6th Symphony, and as he said himself in an interview 'we all, students and teachers alike, went mad about it'. Several years later came *The Rite of Spring*; Stravinsky's immensely powerful evocation of a remote and sinister past moved Ireland deeply. But though he admired the clear, hard outlines and the driving rhythms of Stravinsky's music, you will look in vain for any obvious traces of the Russian master's style in Ireland's work. Composers like Stravinsky were not influences in the sense of being models to be imitated, but beacons to illuminate the path along which his own true direction lay. Nonetheless, the kinship can be clearly heard in the pithy motives and nervous rhythms with which Ireland's overture *Satyricon* begins.

Another work inspired by Petronius' Latin novel is the one-movement *Fantasy Sonata* for clarinet and piano; in its quieter and more meditative passages this lovely piece shows Ireland's affinity with the music of French Impressionism, the second of the two counter-influences which helped to free him from the Brahmsian straight-jacket. Of all his French contemporaries Ireland preferred Ravel, and always spoke of his music with deep understanding and affection. Ireland, incidentally, was the pianist in the first English performance of Ravel's Trio; to make sure that the occasion should be worthy of the work, Ireland insisted — so the players subsequently calculated — on 35 rehearsals. (It is as well to remember that Ravel was not an actual Impressionist; like Ireland himself, he was a classicist using Impressionist techniques.)

Next to Ravel, John Ireland held Debussy in the highest esteem. In 1941 he wrote to me about the first performance of a violin concerto by a British composer, sympathising with him because Debussy's *Nocturnes* had been played immediately before the première of the new piece: '... hardly a good choice to precede a new work — few, if any, modern works could have stood up to them.' Exciting though these new musical experiences, Russian and French, were to Ireland, and helpful as signposts directing him along his own individual path, the composer never fell into the trap of cutting himself off from his roots. In particular, he never forgot the lessons learnt during his student days at the Royal College. 'Stanford could be severely critical, almost cruel at times', Ireland once told an interviewer. (A characteristic verdict on an apprentice quartet was 'dull as ditchwater, my boy'.) 'His best quality as a teacher was that he made you feel that nothing but the best would do.' Such was the impression Stanford made on Ireland as teacher and composer, that he kept his photograph by him for the rest of his life.

So much for the make-up of Ireland's musical language; to what purpose was it put? And what were the non-musical sources of Ireland's inspiration? These latter were many and various: English poetry; a feeling for place, or rather places; and that very rare thing, a sense of the immanence of the past — in other words a past so close to the present as to be immediately perceptible by any sensitive person on the look-out for it. It was this quality which he recognised and responded to in Stravinsky's *Rite of Spring*, and he also found it one memorable day in 1906 at Charing Cross, when he bought from the station bookstall a copy of Arthur Machen's *The House of Souls*. Machen is a writer seldom read nowadays — except perhaps by enthusiasts for John Ireland's music; but his tales of other worlds and other days are filled with so powerful a sense of the supernatural that an impressionable reader like myself is frequently reduced to terror or, in the more emotional stories, to tears. Ireland's *Legend* for piano and orchestra is perhaps the finest, certainly the most extended, work written under Machen's influence, and it is dedicated to the author. The central section embodies a strange Machen-like experience: in Julian Herbage's words, 'the composer had taken a picnic lunch to a favourite spot on the Downs, but had scarcely un-packed it before he was conscious of some children dancing in front of him. He at first thought they were real, but then he noticed their archaic clothing. He glanced away for an instant, and when he looked back the children had vanished.'

So far as I know Ireland never set any of Machen's words to music, though he used them as an epigraph for his piano piece *The Scarlet Ceremonies*. Of the many poets to whom Ireland went for his song texts, the one with whom he was most in sympathy was A E Housman. There are fine settings of Housman by other composers — Vaughan Williams' cycle *On Wenlock Edge* is, deservedly, the most familiar; but in none of them can one find that total identification of poet and musician which is the hallmark of Ireland's work. The gritty, grimly humorous, pessimistic and cantankerous Housman spoke straight to the composer's heart, and he responded with two masterpieces, *The Land of Lost Content* and *We'll to the woods no more*. The first of these two cycles is the better known, thanks to a splendid recording made by Peter Pears and Benjamin Britten, but the second is even more remarkable. There are only three movements, the third of which, astonishingly, is for piano alone. The title-song is so tense and emotional — an emotion all the more poignant because expressed with the utmost concision and restraint — that Ireland himself in later years could scarcely bring himself to listen to it. When I wanted to include it in a broadcast he urged me to use the second song, *In boyhood*, instead. Not, he hastened to add, that he regarded it as inferior: 'I consider *In boyhood* a very fair song, and fully expressive of the essential Housman, as far as is possible in such a short space.' Two interesting cross-references are to be found in the first song: to the slow movement of the Piano Sonatina and (in anticipation) to the finale of the Piano Concerto.

For the text of another major work, the *Five Songs* for baritone and piano, Ireland turned to the poems of Thomas Hardy, in which he also found a resignation to fate but considered more profoundly than in Housman's poetry; and it was of course Hardy country which inspired the symphonic rhapsody for orchestra, *Mai Dun*. But despite the attraction of Dorset's ancient history, three other places had a more lasting effect on John Ireland's music: the Channel Islands, Sussex and London.

A glance through the solo piano music (recently published in a collected edition) immediately shows this three-fold influence at work. To Jersey we owe *The Island Spell*, a piece which exultantly celebrates the composer's emancipation from the grip of German music, and to nearby Guernsey the magnificent three-movement cycle *Sarnia*. Sussex was a particularly happy place for Ireland; after the war he lived in retirement there in a converted windmill facing Chanctonbury Ring, and during his creative years he drew inspiration from the Downs for *Equinox, Amberley Wild Brooks* and the massive Piano Sonata. It may seem surprising that such a lover of the country could respond equally readily to the moods of a big city. (His pupil Britten could not endure London after East Anglia.) Ireland's long residence in Chelsea, however, had taught him to appreciate the strange fascination and curiously beautiful ugliness of the city scene. One consequence was the *Ballade of London Nights*, a work put aside for revision and never published during the composer's lifetime, which has since been posthumously edited by one of his most sympathetic interpreters, Alan Rowlands. Fine though it is, it cannot compare with the *London Pieces*, which were completed in 1920. The three movements are, in reverse order, an atmospheric evocation of *Soho Forenoons; Ragamuffin*, perhaps a portrait of one of the local boys — 'grubby but beautiful' as Ireland put it — who belonged to his church choir; and a barcarolle, *Chelsea Reach*. This, with its haunting melody, perpetually shifting piano textures and impressive command of large-scale musical design, is unquestionably a masterpiece.

John Ireland made an outstanding contribution to English music in three media in particular: songs, piano and chamber music. In this respect he reminds one of Fauré, and indeed he is to be spoken of in the same terms as the great French master. Like Fauré he wrote comparatively seldom for larger forces, but with great effect whenever he did so; Fauré's gentle *Requiem* is matched by Ireland's incisive *These things shall be.* Unlike the Frenchman, Ireland wrote nothing for the theatre; he did, however, write incidental music for a radio production of *Julius Caesar* and for the film *The Overlanders*, scores which have recently been arranged in a form which makes them suitable for concert performance.

The pride and joy of all who love Ireland's music, however, is the Piano Concerto, written in 1930. This shows many facets of the composer's art that I have not yet touched on: his skill at motivic development — all the passionate outpourings of the opening movement derive from the first five simple crotchets; the incisiveness of his orchestration; and his marvellous economy and sense of timing. What other composer, having created the great arch of melody that begins the slow movement, could have refrained from repeating it later once or even twice in its entirety? Ireland is content merely to recall half-a-dozen bars. And when, reluctantly, we are awakened from the dream world of the slow movement by the entry of the timpani — the drums have been silent up to now, held in reserve for this special purpose — there is compensation in the shape of one of Ireland's happiest melodic inventions. (This has a tick-tock accompaniment marvellously evocative of the spirit of Joseph Haydn — himself a Londoner by adoption.) The personal and the popular are so well blended in this concerto that it would not be out of place to apply to it Mozart's own self-analysis: 'There are passages here and there from which connoisseurs alone can derive satisfaction; but these passages are written in such a way that the less learned cannot fail to be pleased, though without knowing why.'

In 1958, after hearing the first LP recording of the concerto, with Colin Horsley as the soloist, I wrote to John Ireland to express (not for the first time) my enthusiasm for the work. His reply shows the concern which most composers feel about changing public attitudes to their music:

My dear Geoffrey,
    So many thanks for your kind, generous letter. I value very highly your appreciation of my concerto. Coming from a musician of your generation and high standing it is indeed heartening and encouraging to one whose music is not in the current fashion. Some writer in *The Times* said it was like very sweet marsala as compared with the 'dry Burgundy' quality of Stravinsky's *Capriccio*, which occupies the other side of the record. In the 1940s the late James Agate found it so dissonant and ugly that he almost refused to speak to me again! He regarded it as a personal insult ...
    Your old friend
    John Ireland

He need not have worried about the shifts in musical taste where his concerto was concerned. If there is ever going to be any future at all for British music, Ireland's concerto will (without any doubt whatever) be part of it.

PART III

16. When I did muse in boyhood

Shortly after my eighth birthday and, as P G Wodehouse would say, without any previous training or experience, I found myself a member of the choir of Salisbury Cathedral. How this happened I have no idea. Of course I remember vividly — or have convinced myself that I remember, which amounts to the same thing — the various hoops which had to be jumped through: eating formal lunch with a terrifyingly large (though otherwise kindly) headmaster, taking a series of musical tests set by the sub-organist, and listening to a commercial recording which had just been made by the choir. This last was an ironical touch, because one side of the record was devoted to a composer on whose secular music I was to devote much editorial energy and enthusiasm later in life: Sterndale Bennett.

What I cannot remember is why my mother entered me for the choir in the first place. We were not a family of musicians, and I have no recollection of exhibiting any signs of incipient musical talent before coming to Salisbury. Nor did I exhibit any on the day of the test, according to the sub-organist — who was wont to declare that my admission was due to no merits of my own, but entirely to his instinct and perspicacity.

Be that as it may, I was to spend the next five years of my life (except for rather less than eight weeks' holiday a year) within a stone's-throw of Salisbury Cathedral. Even those who have never been there will surely know it from pictures. Not only does the building possess the tallest and most elegant of English spires, but thanks to the founder, Bishop Poore, it has sufficient open green space on all sides to allow the spectator to stand back and appreciate it. The interior of the cathedral is felt by some to be austere and disappointing; certainly it suffered from the loss of its mediaeval stained glass and from the monstrous ravages of James Wyatt, the architect who was commissioned to restore the cathedral in conformity with late 18th-century taste. But to *know* the interior of Salisbury Cathedral, to live with it as opposed to casually visiting it, is in the end to love it.

The school and its cricket field both lay within the walled boundaries of the Close; the school garden backed on the River Avon, where we punted, bathed, and by special permission occasionally fished. (I can only recall one angling success: a friend of mine caught and shared a very succulent eel.) To live, to sing, to study, to play games in such surroundings at such an impressionable age was an overwhelming experience.

Besides becoming a five-year fixture in Salisbury Close, I now found myself part of a carefully constituted hierarchy. At the top was the Bishop's Boy, or Head Chorister. It was his duty to escort the Bishop whenever the latter attended Divine Service in the Cathedral, wearing as his badge of office a purple tassel on his mortar-board. There were 15 other full choristers, the senior of whom were responsible for putting the markers in the music books for next day's services. All 15 were distinguished from the half-a-dozen juniors who were still learning their job — the probationers — by black tassels on their mortar-boards. Every choirboy wore Eton jacket, waistcoat and long trousers, with a ruff instead of collar and tie. This absurd costume has left me in later life with such a loathing for formal wear that I can be induced to put on my solitary suit only for occasions of peculiar importance, and even then primarily to avoid domestic displeasure. Nowadays, of course, Eton suits have been dispensed with, and ruffs are put on with cassocks — at service time only.

Next in the hierarchy came the other pupils, non-singing boarders and day boys whom we, the élite, tolerated but (unless they were good at cricket) despised. We took a still more extreme view of our contemporaries outside the Close, and for some reason regarded the boys of Bishop Wordsworth's School with particular animosity. A view from the other side of the wall would have been a salutary corrective to our self-esteem. In *The Lord of the Flies*, you will recall, it is the choirboys who are depicted as the ring-leaders in every kind of devilment and destruction. And the author of that terrifying masterpiece, William Golding, was once a master at Bishop Wordsworth's School.

Our life centred round the Cathedral and its music. We marched two by two in our mortar-boards across the Close to the organist's house for one hour's rehearsal every weekday; Mattins and Evensong were sung daily in the Cathedral except for Wednesday and Monday morning, no matter how minuscule the congregation; and on Sunday morning Mattins was immediately followed by Sung Eucharist. The Cathedral organist in charge of the music was Doctor, later Sir Walter, Alcock. His aristocratic manner was not universally popular in the Close, but we boys adored him. As soon as he appeared in person to take our practice, instead of delegating it to his assistant, we immediately greeted him with a deafening shout of 'Good-morning, Doctor!' — to which his invariable response was a hand cupped round his ear and the barely audible question 'Did anybody speak?'

He was without doubt the greatest organ-player of his day; to see him sitting still as a stone while he steered his vast instrument through the polyphonic mazes of a Bach fugue was an object lesson in obtaining the maximum of result with the minimum of effort. And it was legendary that he always had leisure to shake the hand of any old chorister who appeared in the organ-loft, even if he was in the throes of a four-part stretto at the time. Such was the power of his musical personality that the choir — six professionals as well as us boys — were effortlessly and totally under his control. I remember only two exceptions to this general rule. One Evensong every single thing went wrong; the unaccompanied responses sounded out of tune, the amens were ragged, the solo boy missed his entry in the Magnificat and the anthem came irretrievably to pieces in the middle. Retribution inevitably followed: after the service Sir Walter appeared at the vestry door and ordered us all back to the choirstalls, where, in deep disgrace, we had to go through the whole of Evensong again from beginning to end.

The second episode was, to us boys at any rate, exceedingly hilarious. We were singing one of those glorious anthems of Purcell where the bass soloist has to rise from the middle to the top of his compass through a succession of slowly mounting semitones. By some mischance the Decani bass, a man with a very powerful voice, got one semitone out. As a delicate hint that he should fall in line, Sir Walter pulled out a louder stop. Resenting the interference, or perhaps regarding it as mistaken, the soloist sang his next semitone rather louder. Sir Walter played the correct semitone louder still. Nothing daunted, the soloist took a deep breath and sang his next wrong note with even louder volume, and so the two contestants proceeded up the scale an excruciating semitone apart, each trying unavailingly to drown the other. The post-mortem must have been held after we left the vestry, for we never heard Sir Walter's comments. No doubt they were considered unsuitable for our delicate ears.

Friday evening was an important occasion, because on our way out of Evensong we usually caught our first glimpse of the new service-sheets listing the music to be sung during the following week. We had strong likes and dislikes; bearing the limitations of age in mind, our taste was (I think) pretty sound. We were too young to appreciate the austerities of Tallis' Service in the Dorian Mode, but we revelled in the vitality of Gibbons' *Hosanna to the Son of David*. Purcell's *Bell Anthem* was a favourite, even without the benefit of an orchestra for the symphonies — though it was hard to remain silent while the alto, tenor and bass stole most of the glorious limelight. In general we liked any music which generated a sense of excitement, such as the closing chorus of Elgar's *Light of the World*. A powerful organ part was always a plus value; but if the music was vivid enough — a good example being Samuel Wesley's motet *In exitu Israel* — we could happily dispense with an accompaniment. Worthy but pedestrian settings of the canticles by minor composers of the baroque were our *bête noir*. I remember that when someone pasted a sticker on the front cover of Travers in F reading 'Given away free with Meccano Magazine', we all felt that this was the best thing that could possibly be done with it.

The abiding impression that has remained with me as the result of five years spent singing Anglican church music is the amazing strength and continuity of the English tradition. Most people look at our history as they look at an Underground poster which has been through the hands of a graffiti artist — half the lady's teeth have been blacked out. For them, there is nothing of significance between Purcell and Elgar. No cathedral chorister would ever make such an ignorant mistake. Every age had its own masterpieces to contribute to our repertory, which stretched in an unbroken line from the Tudor polyphonists to the present day.

Apart from the occasional anthem or canticle setting which happened to strike us as objectionable, there were only two disagreeable aspects of our Cathedral duties. The first was the Sunday sermons. To make sure that we were not getting up to mischief under cover of the choir stalls, we were obliged to march out and sit directly in front of the pulpit under the preacher's eye. If the sermon was dull — the normal occurrence — there was nothing to do to pass the time but add up all the numbers on the hymn-board and factorise the total. On Fridays the Litany was always sung at the end of Mattins. This could be beguiled by timing the celebrant, and there was always the intriguing possibility that a few seconds might be nipped off the shortest recorded time, which was something around 12 minutes or, less agreeably, added to the longest, which was over 16. The long-distance record holder was a certain venerable minor canon whom otherwise we admired for his treasure-hunting activities — he had devoted a lifetime to prospecting for the remains of the cathedral's lost mediaeval glass. But his interminably slow and nasal delivery of the Litany drove us to distraction, as it did — we were delighted to discover one morning — the rest of the clergy. That Friday, as the minor canon was slowly processing from his distant choir-stall to the prayer desk in front of the nave, one of the canons-in-residence decided he could bear it no longer. Abruptly leaping out of his seat, he won the race to the prayer desk by a short head; and as he triumphantly began the Litany with our most enthusiastic musical and spiritual support, the rightful celebrant was obliged to retrace his steps in disconsolate silence back to his own stall.

Sermons and Litanies were more than compensated for by periodic special events, such as a complete performance of Mendelssohn's *Lobgesang* Choral Symphony. Best of all we enjoyed linking up with the local choral society for Bach's B minor Mass, not only because of the excitement of being near an orchestra full of exotic instruments like the corno di caccia, but also because it meant staying up well past bed-time for the dress rehearsal. Each summer we joined the choirs of Winchester and Chichester Cathedrals for a festival service — in recent years this has grown into a whole week of music-making, known as the Southern Cathedrals' Festival. If the service was on home ground, *we* had the privilege of providing the soloists; but there was plenty of compensation for an away fixture, including the coach trip, generous hospitality, and seeing how the other half lived. We were very awed when the Chichester boys assured us that singing mistakes were regularly rewarded with a good beating in the vestry immediately after the service. In retrospect I am sure this was pure fiction, made up to imbue us with a sense of their own importance. Had it been true, however, the mingling of organ voluntary and juvenile lamentation would have produced a curious anticipation of Maurizio Kagel's *Fantasie for organ with obbligati*, in which the composer combines organ music with a tape of sound effects taken from the organist's everyday life.

I recall a personal disaster during this same Chichester visit. It was a hot day, and as we processed round the cathedral singing the opening hymn, I put my hand in my pocket to take out my handkerchief. Instead of the handkerchief I encountered a glutinous brown mess, the liquified remains of a bar of chocolate which I had bought earlier in the day, put in my pocket and forgotten; so that I was, in every sense, stuck with it until the end of the service.

All the musical events which I have been describing had to be fitted into the ordinary school curriculum. This didn't leave us much spare time except on Saturday afternoons; on the other hand, neither games nor work seemed to suffer. One year we fielded an unbeaten cricket team throughout the season; and when I left the choir school with two companions in July 1933, all three of us had won scholarships in academic subjects (not music) to help pay for the next stage of our education.

The chief architect of these successes was a new headmaster, who had been appointed to take charge of the school in the term immediately following my arrival there. He raised the academic standard of the school beyond recognition; moreover, he had a real flair for choosing assistant members of staff. Two of these I remember with particular gratitude — his deputy, known to all and sundry as Mr Griff, and the history master, Michael Gilbert. Mr. Griff was a real father-figure — every evening his study would be crawling with small boys, reading his books and, in my case, playing his gramophone records. As for Michael, his first detective story, *Close Quarters*, draws on his experiences at the school, though if you want the cream of Gilbert I think I would recommend two later thrillers, set in Italy: *Death in Captivity* and *The Etruscan Net*. The new headmaster had, in fact, every gift except one; tragically (since it was the only failing calculated to disqualify him from looking after children in any circumstances whatever) he could not control his temper. He also had a profound belief in the wisdom of military men. Thanks to the imbecile advice of a retired colonel who believed that all boys ought to be toughened up, we were never allowed to wear gloves even in the depth of winter. We were also compelled to play rugby football when the ground was frozen solid — imagine taking such insane risks with the hands of potential professional musicians — and in summer we were taught to swim (or in my case, not to swim) by being thrown from the bank into the river. It was one of the red-letter days of my life when I returned to the school after a brief absence spent sitting for a scholarship, to discover that he had been asked to leave, and — a happy ending if ever there was one — that our beloved Mr Griff had been appointed in his place.

There were usually a few days when we had to be in Salisbury in order to sing at the Cathedral either before the boarders and dayboys had materialised or after they had disappeared into decent obscurity. These 'choristers hols', as they were known (because although we were living in the school there were no lessons), were far and away the most enjoyable part of our year. Christmas was the tops, with carol singing, shopping in the town and parties; and top of the parties was the one given by Canon Myers. Besides being exceedingly sumptuous, it had the nature of a familiar ritual. There were always presents, there was always the same menu for lunch, and after lunch the canon used always to read us the same story. Once upon a time there were 40 wise men, each of whom had a goat which produced just enough milk every day to keep them alive. To test their resourcefulness the Caliph commanded them to present him on the first of the following month with a bottle of milk each, so that he could take a milk bath. On the fateful day the 40 wise men duly shuffled in with their bottles, but each showed a singular reluctance to accept the honour of starting the proceedings. At last they agreed to stand in a circle round the bath, and at the word of command they began to pour simultaneously. And lo and behold: the bath was filled with pure cold water, because each of the wise men had reasoned that one bottle of water would never be noticed among 39 bottles of milk. Whereupon the Caliph had them all soundly bastinadoed, and sent them home sadder and, it is to be hoped, wiser men. Although we boys knew exactly what was coming next we never tired of the story, and indeed would have felt cheated if an unfamiliar one had been read instead.

Second only to Christmas in our esteem were the first days of summer. Weather permitting, we played informal games of cricket all day long, with half an eye on the most important fixture of the coming season, the match against the choir of St Paul's Cathedral. Summer ended with another major event, the Old Choristers' Festival. In the schoolroom there was always an impromptu concert, with a programme ranging from early Victorian partsongs to dance music played by the number two pianist of Carroll Gibbons' Savoy Hotel Orpheans. In the Cathedral, Festal Evensong was sung by past and present choristers combined; the service was attended by all available clergy, robed in their most elaborate copes, and culminated in a procession to the High Altar for a performance of Stanford's Te Deum in B flat.

My own strong inclination to music may not have been apparent before I arrived at Salisbury, but it emerged unmistakeably soon after my tenth birthday. From then on I filled dozens of manuscript books with juvenile compositions — by dint of writing each of a series of Anglican chants as a separate unit I managed to reach opus one hundred by the time I was 13. At first all I produced was a series of meaningless jottings, like the pothooks toddlers draw in imitation of their parents' handwriting; but gradually what I wrote started to make a bit of sense. From the first I always took immense trouble over the title pages, modelling them — as indeed the music itself was modelled — on the publications we used daily in the choir. A publisher's name, a price, a university degree for the composer, were of the essence. (The idea of becoming G. Bush, Mus.Bac., or even Mus.Doc., then had a hypnotic fascination for me. Needless to say, by the time childish ambitions were realised, all the glamour had flown out of the window.) One day I was discovered scribbling away by Bernard Rose, later Organist and Informator of the choristers at Magdalen College, Oxford, but then Bishop's Boy. He snatched the manuscript from me — it was a setting of the story of Jonah, as far as I can remember — and played it through to a group of boys standing round the piano. This was, I suppose, the greatest artistic

120

triumph of my life. One of my contemporaries came up to me after-wards and said in hushed tones: 'It sounded like a *real* oratorio'.

Nothing much was done about actually teaching us music. The pro-bationers met together once a week on their own; during these special periods I recall learning all the key signatures by a system of mnemonics, rehearsing a chromatic scale and an octave jump to the words 'I will practise semitones each day till I am PER - FECT', and singing Bach's *My heart ever faithful.* Like all Bach, this was a horribly unvocal piece — not a patch on Handel's *Let the bright seraphim* — but it served to teach us that at a final cadence the seventh was not obliged to rise to the keynote and — by extension — that the rules of musical grammar were made to be broken. Piano lessons were extra. These were given, I am sorry to say, not by an expert but by whoever held the post of sub-organist at the time. If he happened to be a good teacher we prospered; if not, not. There was no provision for any other instrumental tuition, and this I regard as a major deficiency. Nor were there facilities for an appren-tice composer to learn his craft. In my last year I saved three-and-sixpence out of my pocket-money to buy Sir John Stainer's *Harmony*, which I worked through on my own; and once I summoned up the courage to show Sir Walter Alcock what he called 'a little composement' — actually a waltz in C minor, of which I can remember the first eight bars (but fortunately no more) to this day. Sir Walter was kindness itself, but that didn't constitute a lesson. On the other hand, in spite of the absence of formal teaching, we learnt the most prodigious amount simply by *doing.* Music was around us all the time; we absorbed it as children absorb a foreign language when they live abroad, effortlessly. We did not need to be taught, for instance, as some first-year harmony students at university have to be taught, the normal spacing of a succession of 4-part chords; we knew which was the right and which the wrong way just from the look of the page.

Besides writing music myself, I succeeded briefly in persuading some of my friends to do the same. When they had done enough for my pur-poses I carefully copied out their pieces into a manuscript book bought for the occasion. I suppose the idea for this had come to me from monumental collections like Boyce and Greene's *Cathedral Music* which we used in the choir. Be that as it may, this was my first elementary essay in textual editing, a job to which in recent years I have given most of the time I have been able to spare from composition.

An artistic diet consisting exclusively of religious music diluted with the simpler of Beethoven's piano sonatinas would probably not have been very nourishing in the long run; so it was a stroke of luck for me that there was a remarkable boy among the senior choristers who was already familiar with the work of Debussy, Stravinsky and other 'moderns'. By playing me some of Debussy's preludes on the piano, he showed me that there were new musical worlds outside the Cathedral Close waiting to be explored as soon as I should be capable (which I wasn't then) of exploring them. This boy, David Gascoyne, was to become the first, perhaps the only, great surrealist poet which this country has produced; so it is fitting that my chief memory of him should be of an utterly surrealist kind. As a result of spending his entire week's pocket-money on cocoanut ice, he was suddenly taken ill in the middle of Evensong. With astonishing presence of mind he converted his surplice into an impromptu basin, and marched out with the grisly remains held like a collection plate in front of him. This skilful saving of the situation was, unfortunately, not enough to prevent our sweet allowance being cut in half from then on.

Boys have earned their education by singing in Salisbury Cathedral ever since the 12th century. Their fortunes have varied; in the 14th century they were little better than a guild of beggars, whereas by the 16th they were the proud possessors of two milk-producing cows. (Canon Fletcher's history does not relate whether they were ever set a problem similar to that posed by the Caliph to the 40 wise men.) The choristers no longer live beside the River Avon, but are very prosperously housed in the former Bishop's Palace. Throughout the period of its existence the Cathedral has produced its quota of composers, including William Lawes and Michael Wise. Lawes, son of one of the Vicars Choral, was killed in the Civil War at the seige of Chester; Wise, contemporary of Purcell and organist of the Cathedral, was widely known for his anthem *The ways of Zion do mourn* and for his ungovernable temper. (He is said to have once interrupted a sermon of which he had grown weary by striking up the outgoing voluntary, much to the displeasure of Charles II and the delight of the choristers. Unfortunately, just short of his fortieth birthday he rushed out of his house after a quarrel with his wife, knocked down a watchman and had his head split open with a bill-hook.) I hope to avoid the violent end met by both these masters; but the thought that as a former chorister and as the composer of a Salisbury Mass I stand somewhere in their line of musical succession is curiously comforting.

17. Self-portrait

A composer is known by the company he keeps. The simplest way for me to introduce myself is to tell you about the composers who have influenced me, either by their music, their personality, or both.* But first a general word about my schooldays. Their importance is too obvious to need underlining; did not the Jesuits say something to the effect that provided they could keep a child for the first seven years, anyone else could have it for the other seventy?

As I have described elsewhere, my musical life began as a choirboy at Salisbury Cathedral. One of the chief results of this was (I think) a proper understanding of what human voices can or cannot do. Which is the cue for me to criticise some of my contemporaries (and juniors). It is said that dog shouldn't eat dog, but since I am very partial to the occasional slice of dog I shan't let that deter me. Many contemporary composers, I feel, sit down at their pianos and play a nice, clear, striking dissonance. This they then incorporate into a piece for unaccompanied choir. They ignore the fact that such a dissonance may be extremely difficult to sing and require endless (expensive) rehearsal. This wouldn't matter so much — I am all for giving singers hell from time to time — if the results of giving the singers hell were reasonably effective; but they aren't. Complex dissonances become blurred when sung because of the conflicting vibrations set up when human voices compete against one another; the amorphous mass of sound resulting from the notes an inexperienced composer has written could equally well, perhaps even better, be produced by a random collection of notes picked out blindfold with the aid of a pin.

When I went on from Salisbury to Lancing College I was exceptionally lucky; first of all in our music master, Jasper Rooper, himself a composer of some fine choral pieces. Jasper Rooper did not teach us — he did better than that: he made us teach ourselves. If we were composers, he encouraged us to write within existing school resources and performed the results at school concerts; if we were organists, he allowed us to accompany the chapel services; if we had ambitions to conduct, he showed us the basic technique and then let us loose on the school orchestra. He always proceeded to criticise what we did — but as an equal, as one musician to another.

* To avoid duplication, I have omitted all reference to John Ireland.

Secondly, Jasper Rooper had been a pupil of Vaughan Williams, and one day by arrangement he took me over to see him and show him what I had written. I was a little bit frightened of VW when he first appeared — he seemed so huge, like a vast, unshaven bear; he had no collar and tie on, and was shambling around in bedroom slippers, looking several sizes larger than life. Needless to say he was the opposite of terrifying; he was kindness itself, giving up a whole afternoon (and remember, time is perhaps a composer's most precious possession) to toil through a lot of juvenile rubbish. One comment I have never forgotten: 'Don't be afraid of writing a tune, then stopping it and starting another. The critics won't like it, but that's the way to write music.' There is a double implication here, of course; first that a composer should keep to the point and not waste time on transitions or unnecessary filling-in passages, and secondly that he should try to make his thematic material as striking and memorable as possible.

The results of this visit to Vaughan Williams were visible for a long time. I studied the Fourth Symphony (then new) until I knew it almost by heart, and I wrote an organ piece full of chains of triads, all of which were subsequently blue-pencilled as forbidden consecutives (believe it or not) by the examiner for Higher Certificate Music to whom it was submitted. (I retained sufficient fondness for this piece to rewrite and publish it many years later under the title *Toccata.*)

VW's advice reminds me of another truly perceptive remark made to me (much later in my career) by Benjamin Frankel, whom I consulted on the advice of friends when I was feeling particularly depressed about my lack of musical progress. The gist of my complaint to him was that I seemed to be able to write nothing but tunes, and that matters requiring real resource, like counterpoint, were quite beyond me. He thought for a bit, and then said: 'Are you sure you have diagnosed your problem correctly? Oughtn't you to be worrying about the things you *can* do rather than the things you can't do? Are the tunes you are writing really good enough? [He was correct: they weren't.] Concentrate on what you need, and leave counterpoint alone until it becomes relevant to what you want to write'. This is only a summary of his remarks, but they constitute what seems to me in retrospect, as indeed it did at the time, to be wonderfully sound advice. As far as I myself am concerned, compositional techniques cannot be acquired in a vacuum. As the need to use counterpoint more extensively has increased (in recent works like my two piano sonatinas), so has the ability to handle it more freely.

In 1938 I went up to Balliol as Nettleship Scholar in classics and composition. As far as music was concerned I was left to fend for myself;

but luckily Tom (now Sir Thomas) Armstrong, who was in charge of most of Oxford's performing activities, believed that apprentice composers should be given every chance to hear their own work. He once astonished the University orchestra by stopping the rehearsal of a Fauré suite, peering into the dim distance towards the back desk of the second violins (which I shared with the future Lord Bishop of Portsmouth) and inviting me to write a piece on similar lines for them to play. (The two of us were allowed to scrape away at rehearsals provided we did not disgrace the orchestra by actually appearing at concerts; but even this limited experience of orchestral playing from the inside proved very helpful to me.) All that remains of this particular project is a single movement scored not for orchestra but for two pianos: *An Oxford Scherzo*. I did, however, complete a piece for string orchestra in which I tried to incorporate a musical experience which had just made a great impression on me: walking across the quad one day I heard, through adjoining windows, a Bach concerto and a Sydney Bechet blues played simultaneously on two different gramophones. This Concertino (there were solo parts for two violins) was played under Tom's direction at one of the Balliol concerts. Had I then been familiar with the music of Charles Ives I might have brought it off; but for want of adequate technique the piece was a failure and I later destroyed it.

It was at another Balliol concert that I first met John Gardner, then organ scholar of Exeter College and my senior by three years. I was much impressed by his personality, his fluency, and by the success he had already achieved (a string quartet of his was broadcast from Paris, followed by a vodka party which made me iller than I have ever been in my life); but I was even more impressed by the unaffected lyricism of his music, which encouraged me to make my first serious attempt at song-writing. This form of composition — of which more later — was eventually to become my obsession.

The examiner for my scholarship had been Ernest Walker, the first truly great historian of English music — perhaps indeed the only one to date, since all his judgements (agree with them or not) were based on first-hand pioneering research. To him I owed my introduction to Margaret Deneke of Lady Margaret Hall, tireless patron of Oxford music — and to her, one of the most unusual experiences of my musical life, which I have often thought of writing up under the title *An afternoon at Madame Verdurin's*. This featured a performance of Schubert's F minor Fantasia by Donald Tovey (first holder, incidentally, of the Nettleship Scholarship) and Benjamin Britten, who had come over to spend the day at the Denekes' summer home in Southwold. (I had been invited

for a week's seaside holiday; two other composers, Ernest Walker himself and Bernard Naylor, were also in residence). Tovey was then in the last year of his life, his hands so crippled by rheumatism that a piano with smaller keys than usual had been specially built for him, to enable him to go on performing in public. After the Schubert I was invited to play through a recently completed *Te Deum* of my own which Ernest thought would interest Tovey; in typical undergraduate fashion I ignored the opinions of my seniors and opted instead to play a rather flashy set of variations which I hoped (in vain) would impress Benjamin Britten.*
I also disgraced myself by giggling when Tovey — unaccustomed to listen to anyone else, but having run out of pronouncements of his own — gave an imitation of the trumpets of Tutenkhamen followed by an unsolicited reading from a book of German poetry. This scene had decided elements of Proustian comedy; but despite a touch of vulgarity Margaret Deneke was far too warm, too generous and musically sensitive to be cast as the heartless and hypocritical Madame Verdurin, and so the article has remained unwritten.

Some critics have professed to find traces of Britten's influence in my songs (which I shall discuss later). Rather, I believe that any resemblances are to be traced back to a common source — Henry Purcell, the model *par excellence* for anyone attempting to set the English language to music. In this connection I would like to quote a very perceptive sentence from Gerald Abraham:

> 'We forget that in a sense a creative artist chooses his influences. An influence cannot make itself felt deeply unless it corresponds to something in himself'.

This of course explains why you will hear nothing from me (as you probably would from most of my contemporaries and juniors) about Schoenberg. This does not constitute a value-judgement about Schoenberg's music; it just means that there is nothing in him or his work which corresponds to me at all. I find his clotted textures and furrowed brow utterly antipathetic. Unlike the music of his pupil Webern, Schoenberg's compositions (with very few exceptions) never give me room to breathe. Putting on another hat for a moment and becoming a historian, I would like to add the further comment that the influence of Germany on English music during the past two centuries has been almost wholly bad. We already have an inborn tendency to be ponderous and boring without any outside assistance; what we need is something to bring out the lighter

---

* I had already met Britten, thanks to Peter Pears and the Lancing connection. He too was good enough later on to spend an afternoon going through various compositions and making penetrating comments; at the time I found his undiluted criticism rather too stiff a dose to swallow. But he had a kind word for my unaccompanied setting of Shelley's *Music, when soft voices die.*

and more mercurial side of our musical character — the sort of stimulus Purcell found in the Italian music of his day. The list of German composers who have overshadowed English music makes depressing reading — depressing because each successive generation has seemed incapable of learning from its predecessors' mistakes. First there was Handel; then Mendelssohn; then Brahms — the great bearded figure of Brahms; then, after a brief interlude during which VW temporarily liberated us, the sequence was resumed with Schoenberg and Stockhausen, and shows no sign of coming to a conclusion.

Now after all those generalities I would like to discuss a few specific works which have had a formative effect on me, starting with Prokofiev's 3rd Piano Concerto. I didn't understand a note of it when it was broadcast from the Proms one school holidays, but it knocked me sideways all the same. Repeated hearings thrilled me even more, and when soon afterwards I was given a recording of the *Classical Symphony*, I became a Prokofiev fan for life. Between them these two works illustrate all the many different facets of Prokofiev's style — the clarity of texture and mastery of form; the love of sudden harmonic sidesteps, such as the one with which he wittily ends the Gavotte of the *Classical Symphony*; the marvellous melodic invention, so warm in the finale of the 3rd Piano Concerto and so cool in the central variations; the driving energy of the toccata-like scales which dominate the first movement of the concerto; and throughout the sense of humour, sometimes gently ironic, sometimes sarcastic, sometimes harshly grotesque.

It is probably unnecessary to mention Prokofiev's mastery of his own instrument, the piano, both in its percussive and romantic aspects; but I would like to draw your attention to the extraordinarily economical brilliance of his orchestration. Every instrument is used in its most effective register; at climaxes there is always a tremendously wide spectrum of sound, with the basses placed at the bottom and the violins at the top of their compass. At the same time there are no wasted notes, there is no unnecessary complexity. On paper it all looks disarmingly simple. Consider the stunning end of the first movement of the 3rd Piano Concerto; open the score and what catches your eye? Several bars of tied semibreves for the brass in the middle of the page. Not very exciting, surely ... yet in practice the roof nearly caves in. The end of the *Classical Symphony* comes off like a rocket too, and that uses only a modest Mozartian orchestra.

Whether Prokofiev the man was as attractive as his music I am inclined to doubt. Judging from the autobiographical fragments and reminiscences which have been published I should think he may well have been rather a self-centred man, difficult to deal with and impervious to other people's feelings. On the other hand, I can't help admiring his efficiency, his resolute punctuality, his love of playing games and still more his love of winning them (just like me), and the single-hearted pursuit of perfection which frequently compelled him to dismantle and reconstruct even published works.

My desire to emulate Prokofiev can be most easily seen, as you might expect, in my early work, especially in my overture *The Rehearsal*, which was sketched in 1943 and orchestrated in 1945. The title refers to a play by the Restoration dramatist the Duke of Buckingham, in which Dryden and the heroic semi-operas of the day were satirised, rather as Sheridan lampooned his fellow playwrights in *The Critic*. It has been, and still is, given quite a number of performances, including one at the Cheltenham Festival of 1953, which suggests that it hasn't at any rate fallen too far short of its model. If I listen to it on a day when I am feeling particularly optimistic, I even think Prokofiev might quite have liked it himself.

My *Concerto for Light Orchestra*, commissioned by the BBC for their 1958 Light Music Festival, and my *Whydah Variations* for two pianos, commissioned in 1961 by the Redcliffe Festival (now the Redcliffe Concerts of British Music), are much less obviously derivative, but show that I have profited from studying Prokofiev's use of both orchestra and piano. Prokofiev's influence is finally assimilated, I believe, in the Wind Quintet written in 1963 for the New London Wind Ensemble and dedicated to the composer's memory. In this work I hope and think that I have managed to convey something of the spirit of Prokofiev while writing in a style entirely my own. The result is neither gay nor sad, neither witty nor serious, neither lyrical nor forceful, but all these things by turn and sometimes simultaneously. My increasing concern with counterpoint is evident in the slow movement, which rather unusually combines the elements of fugue and funeral march. All in all, I believe this to be my most important chamber-music work to date.

Another exciting discovery of my early teens was Constant Lambert's *The Rio Grande*. By this time I was in the sixth form at school and had graduated to what was laughingly called a study, that is to say a small cupboard with a skylight into which it was just possible to squeeze a table, a chair, and a portable gramophone I had carried off from home without asking. I had just bought the 78 rpm recording of Lambert's work (a wonderful performance with Lambert conducting and Hamilton Harty playing the solo piano part) as the inevitable consequence of singing it the previous term in the school choral society under Jasper Rooper. Whenever I had a spare moment I played the record full blast with the skylight open and terrorized the other inhabitants of the corridor.

(If I'd had five pounds for every time I played it, I too could have been one of those composers who live happily ever after on islands in the Mediterranean).

Few works could stand up to this sort of treatment, yet *The Rio Grande* thrills me today as much as when I first heard it; I still marvel at the clarity and effectiveness of the scoring, the vivid contrasts of mood, the pungent themes (especially the first chorus entry 'By the Rio Grande They dance no sarabande'), and the vitality of the rhythms imported from North and South American popular music. Later on I came to know Lambert's other jazz-orientated works; the finale of the Piano Concerto written in memory of Heseltine-Warlock is one of the saddest things in all music, and I am always moved when I play the little *Elegaic Blues* for piano, written in memory of Florence Mills. Later still I came to admire many other products of Lambert's extraordinarily versatile genius: his edition of William Boyce's symphonies (a landmark in its day, even though it doesn't measure up to the requirements of current scholarship), his direction of the Sadler's Wells Ballet, and that slaughter-house for sacred cows, his book *Music, Ho!*

Lambert died in 1951, a prematurely old and disappointed man, just after his last work, the ballet *Tiresias*, had been cruelly savaged by the critics. A short while previously I saw and heard him conduct Purcell's *Fairy Queen* at Covent Garden (perhaps I should say half the *Fairy Queen* because it was a sadly truncated affair, though what survived of the opera was splendidly done). Lambert looked like death as he hobbled into the orchestra pit on two sticks and his hand shook as he picked up the baton, but with the first notes of the overture he seemed to come to life again and to be in complete control of both music and the musicians.

Although I never knew him, Constant Lambert had contributed so much to my musical life that I heard the announcement of his death on the radio with a sense of personal shock, and within a few hours there had come to my mind a theme for an elegiac blues in much the same mood as the one he had written for Florence Mills. This eventually became the slow movement of my First Symphony, at which I worked on and off for nearly two years. In the coda the cellos play the first choral entry of *The Rio Grande* in counterpoint with the second subject of the slow movement on the upper woodwind (the quotation is unmistakeable). This slow movement is flanked by two fast ones, both of which gave me any amount of trouble. Despite (or, paradoxically, because of) all the re-writing I had to do the symphony sounds remarkably spontaneous, and it was well received at its first performance at the 1954 Cheltenham Festival (excellently conducted by Rudolf Schwarz) and in 1958 at the

London Proms. Several other performances have been given, despite the fact that getting a hearing for a symphony by a Living British Composer is rather less easy nowadays than the twelve Labours of Hercules rolled into one.

I would like to end with a word or two about my songs. From the worldly point of view writing songs is an even more futile occupation than writing symphonies; the amateur singer is practically extinct, and those professional singers who are not obsessed with 'Das Lied' get precious few opportunities to give a recital of songs of their own choice. Consequently they are hardly ever on the look-out for new songs; and it is distinctly discouraging for a composer who has written (as I have) nearly a dozen cycles to find, far from having sung them, most singers do not even know that they exist.

Anyone with any sense would give up songwriting entirely under these circumstances; but I am too much of an addict to be sensible. My earliest groups of songs are mostly settings of the classics of English poetry: for instance the *Three Songs of Ben Jonson* of 1952. Choosing familiar words is, however, not altogether wise; too often they have been set already, and it is idle to imagine that Morley, Arne or Warlock can be summarily ejected from the repertory in favour of oneself. But to go to contemporary poetry, as I did when I set four poems by Kathleen Raine under the title *The End of Love* in 1954, is simply to replace one problem with another. Much of the work of the best living poets is entirely self-sufficient and by reason either of its style or subject matter unsuitable for musical setting. Even when satisfactory words are found, difficulties over copyright and the division of royalties are liable to arise which any practical composer is obliged to take into account. Moreover, to couple unknown music to unknown words is to create even more consumer resistance than usual among performers and publishers, and it is not surprising that my Raine songs (though first broadcast in 1956) remained in manuscript for nearly thirty years.

More recently, however, I have been lucky enough to discover a middle way. In 1959 I found the words for a cycle for soprano and string orchestra, *Songs of Wonder*, in a book of traditional children's verse; I have felt justified in treating them as adult poems because of the strange overtones and mysterious meanings that so many of them contain. I have framed the whole cycle within two versions of *How many miles to Babylon*, the first appearing out of, the second disappearing into, nothing; by this means I have (I hope) created the atmosphere of make-believe which is the essence of these imaginative poems. Though designed for soprano they can be (and have been) equally well sung by a tenor —

better perhaps, because for some unknown reason the average male singer's enunciation is infinitely superior to the average female's. Is this a physiological defect which cannot be eliminated, or is it simply due to bad training?

In 1961 I carried out a project which had been at the back of my mind for many years; that was to present the Decline and Fall of a lover in a series of six poems chosen from the lute-books of Dowland and his contemporaries. Each song depicts a separate stage in the lover's disillusionment, beginning with Hope and Resolution, then moving through Doubt and Jealousy to Grief and finally Despair. My intention was to produce the musical equivalent of a sequence of Hogarth paintings, so naturally I entitled the work *A Lover's Progress*. Since the cycle was intended for a concert at the Festival Hall Recital Room for which I had been promised the services of three outstanding wind players, I wrote it for the unusual combination of tenor, oboe, clarinet and bassoon.

In 1964 I returned, reluctantly at first but as work progressed with enthusiasm, to the piano as the accompanying instrument; this was the result of a commission from Bridport and West Dorset Music Club for a song-cycle for baritone and piano to celebrate the occasion of their one-hundredth concert. An intensive search for words led to a real treasure-trove: a group of poems from the Greek Anthology by Meleager (floruit 160 BC), magnificently translated by the modern American poet and scholar, Dudley Fitts. There are eight songs in the cycle,* and the first seven all deal with Meleager's mistress, Heliodora, who judging from her promiscuity was probably a professional, but had succeeded in enslaving Meleager none the less. Most of the songs are dramatic scenes in miniature. In the fourth, for instance, the poet imagines himself sending a mosquito to buzz a message in Heliodora's ear without disturbing whoever else happens to be in bed with her at the time; if the mosquito is successful in fetching Heliodora, the tiny insect will be 'crowned with a lion's mane and given great Heracles' bludgeon to brandish in his paw' — a ridiculous picture mirrored in the accompaniment. In the fifth song the poet tosses and turns on his bed unable to sleep, imagining Heliodora also awake and thinking of him — until, with a sudden spasm of jealousy he realises she may be enjoying herself with 'a new love, a newer toy'. In his agony he apostrophises the bedside lamp which he had ordered to keep watch on his mistress: 'Did I not set you to guard her? Forbid it, forbid it.'

The eighth and last poem, however, is not about Heliodora and thus

---

* *Greek Love Songs.*

stands apart from the rest. It is Meleager's epitaph which he wrote for his own tomb, and is a sublimely simple and most touching utterance. The piano begins with a bell-like figure repeated three times; then the baritone sings the autobiographical part of the poem entirely unaccompanied. When he reaches the final words, in which the poet bids farewell to the different passers-by, each in their own language, the piano chime is heard again, with just a suggestion of E major as the voice part drops from a B to a G sharp. The last phrase, however, contains a G natural and dies away unresolved into the distance.

Having a particular performer to write for is a tremendous stimulus to song composition. My *Four Songs from Herrick's Hesperides* of 1949 were written for Donald Munro, a New Zealand pupil of Pierre Bernac, with a voice like peaches and cream. (After some years in this country Donald returned home to found the first-ever New Zealand opera company.) More recently my *Five Mediaeval Lyrics* (1970) were composed for John Barrow, a baritone with a fine sense of drama and splendid diction. New directions are not explored in these mediaeval settings; instead, the idiom of the *Greek Love Songs* is used with greater economy and intensity. However, my last completed song-cycle, *A little love music* (1976), does represent a new departure; it is written for soprano and tenor, who sing either separately or together entirely without accompaniment. Like *A Lover's Progress*, it touches on some of the less happy aspects of love, such as jealousy — but only in passing; and it ends with a nursery rhyme which I take to be symbolic of the search for — and discovery of — the ideal human relationship:

This is the key of the kingdom:
In that kingdom is a city,
In that city is a town,
In that town there is a street,
In that street there winds a lane,
In that lane there is a yard,
In that yard there is a house,
In that house there waits a room,
In that room there is a bed,
On that bed there is a basket,
A basket of flowers.

Flowers in the basket,
Basket on the bed,
Bed in the chamber,
Chamber in the house,
House in the weedy yard,
Yard in the winding lane,
Lane in the broad street,
Street in the high town,
Town in the city,
City in the kingdom:
This is the key of the kingdom.

18. Expert witness

In the spring of 1960 I was asked to act as expert witness in a copyright case involving (among others) the publishing firm of Curwen, the Decca record company and Vera Lynn, wartime Forces' Sweetheart. I would like to think that the invitation came to me because I was already well-known to the defendants' solicitors as a reputable and articulate creative musician; more likely they were working alphabetically through the members' list of the Composers Guild of Great Britain, and had found that all the A's were out of town.

I have since been consulted over a great many cases. This is scarcely surprising; astronomical sums are involved when a pop song becomes an international hit, and the creators of such things all tend to use the same tiny musical vocabulary. Few cases reach court, however, and of those that do, the majority end in compromise before the judge delivers his verdict. This is not surprising either, since musical plagiarism is very difficult to prove. To be successful the plaintiff must demonstrate three things: that a *substantial part* of each of the disputed compositions is involved, that there is a very considerable similarity between these parts, and that the defendant had access to the plaintiff's work. Even if all three can be established to the satisfaction of the judge, it is still open to the defendants to plead coincidence, or to claim that the passages complained of were in fact taken from an earlier composition in the public domain — that is to say, one written sufficiently long ago to be out of copyright.

I soon discovered that an expert witness has a dual function. His first job is to examine the musical facts as dispassionately as possible, and to advise the consulting solicitor whether a charge of plagiarism can or cannot in all likelihood be sustained. If on the basis of such an objective report the solicitor decides to continue the action rather than try to reach a compromise, the expert's position suffers a sea-change. While still keeping strictly to the musical facts, he now becomes an advocate who must advise his client on the most persuasive way of presenting his case. If appearing on behalf of the plaintiff, this might involve him in preparing audio-visual aids for use in court — charts indicating the precise extent of the alleged infringement, and tapes bringing into close juxtaposition the relevant sections of the disputed works. The defendants, on the other hand, might need to be advised where best to look for likely non-copyright sources of the musical ideas they were accused of having stolen. (Recently, for example, John Gardner was able to show that the principal rhythmic motif of an all-important drum solo had been exactly anticipated by Johann Strauss in his overture to *Die Fledermaus.*) During the trial he may continue to give counsel any advice on musical matters that is required; but once in the witness-box he must revert to his original role. There his function is to help the judge reach the correct decision on the facts, and any lapse from objectivity may irreparably ruin his reputation — not to mention his client.

As early as my first case I was made aware of the dangers of unwise partisanship. The defendants had, in all innocence, based a pop-song on a traditional Scottish tune, *Westerin' home*, believing it to be non-copyright. However, the plaintiffs claimed that the central section (known in the trade as the 'middle eight') was actually the original copyright work of the arranger, the late Hugh Roberton. A well-known singer, since deceased, gave expert evidence for the plaintiffs. Carried away by his enthusiasm for the Roberton cause, he allowed himself to make the preposterous assertion that traditional folk-singers never sang sevenths (as found in the passage allegedly composed by Roberton) because they were too difficult. Instead, he declared, the seventh was always reached in two easy stages — up an octave first, then down a second. On the way home from the day's hearing I bought a copy of the *Penguin Book of Folksongs*, edited by A L Lloyd and R Vaughan Williams (two unimpeachable authorities). Having marked the many sevenths to be found in the collection I gave it next morning to counsel, who had less than no difficulty in destroying the witness' credibility in cross-examination.

Musical factors by themselves, however, are not necessarily decisive. In the *Westerin' home* case the judge did in fact rule that the disputed song was traditional and therefore non-copyright in its entirety; but his conclusions owed much to the evidence of a number of Scottish pipers, all of whom claimed to have played it in full long before the Roberton arrangement was published. One of them, in answer to a hostile question from plaintiff's counsel, spontaneously added a detail that carried great conviction. In his first year of military service he had often been unhappy, and this was the tune he used to play to himself behind the barracks to cheer himself up. If this was an invention the judge (and I) were taken in by the finest acting performance ever seen outside the professional theatre.

My next major case was also decided by the judge on the basis of a character assessment. The American composer of the song which was the subject of the action went into the box and swore on oath that he had never heard the plaintiff's tune *In a little Spanish town*. As this tune had for years been a dance-band 'standard', and as the defendant had himself spent quite a time as a dance-band player, such a statement seemed scarcely credible; none the less, the witness' open and confident manner persuaded the judge to believe him. Of course he might have appeared a great deal less open and confident had he been subjected to a ruthless cross-examination. Unfortunately our counsel was a last-minute substitute and — not having had sufficient time to acquire an in-depth knowledge of the case — lacked the confidence necessary to mount a really rigorous challenge. The QC originally briefed had of course mastered all the details; but he had unexpectedly been obliged to withdraw — disastrously as it turned out — because the previous case to which he was committed had over-run its allotted time. Our new counsel was that admirable thing, a Mozart opera enthusiast; but though in Busoni's opinion *The Marriage of Figaro* was the greatest score ever composed, it proved an inadequate guide through the dense and savage jungle of popular music.

If the changes and chances of this mortal life provide one good reason for preferring compromise to litigation, expense is another. Legal talent (and bearing in mind the importance of cross-examination, it is advisable to have the best available) costs money, and it costs more money than might have been expected because of the leisurely way in which trials are conducted. When a case begins the relevant passages in all documents, including previously delivered judgements, must be read aloud in open court; this may take the whole of the first morning. The giving of evidence by question and answer while the judge takes notes in longhand is another time-consuming process. The system has two justifications; the first is the old tag, that justice must be seen to be done, and the second is that it works. Perhaps the latter is less to the credit of the system than of the judges administering it. Thanks to a combination of training and intellect, they are usually well able by mid-afternoon to distinguish between the main issues and tempting irrelevancies in a case about which they knew nothing whatever at ten-thirty that same morning.

Another judicial attribute is the ability to learn. A judge in a copyright case may begin by knowing nothing at all about music; but provided the expert witness makes himself clear, he will soon master the principles of musical grammar simply by listening with intense concentration. Hand in hand with concentration go patience and courtesy. In one case the technicalities of notation had to be explained in connection with two sets of comparison charts prepared by the opposing sides; at a quarter-to-one the judge suggested an early lunch-break as 'Dr Bush has had a very difficult pupil this morning.'

In France they order things, if not better, at any rate differently. Their copyright law is more like our patent law (if I understand these correctly). Ownership belongs to the first comer, and it is no defence for the second to prove that he arrived at the same result by an independant creative effort. Their legal procedure also varies, and may involve an informal hearing before a group of musical assessors who have been appointed by the court, not engaged by the solicitors of the rival claimants.

An opportunity to observe French methods in action came in connection with a piece called the *Telstar March*. When I first examined this, I was immediately struck by its resemblance to the refrain of *Rule, Britannia*. Since the composer was being sued by the author of a march written for a film about Napoleon and named after the battle of Austerlitz, everything was set for an international confrontation. The first round was played in Paris, and ended in a convincing win for the home team. For an hour the judge talked and gesticulated, the lawyers talked and gesticulated, and the musical assessors talked and gesticulated — simultaneously. My halting French was quite inadequate for me to feel able to intervene and explain that *Rule, Britannia* was in origin an operatic aria with chorus; and that therefore it was no use looking for the origin of *Telstar* at the beginning of the piece (as the assessors seemed to expect) but at the end. The return match was played at the Law Courts in the Strand. As the leisurely ritual unfolded with only a single speaker allowed to break the all-pervading silence, the French found themselves as mystified in London as we had been in Paris, and about halfway through the trial both sides agreed on a compromise.

The atmosphere at a British copyright action (no wonder it baffled the French) reminds me of nothing so much as a Test match. There are comparable formalities; the framework also is much the same — each side takes it in turn to bat while their opponents, by means of cross-examination, try to bowl them out. As in most Test matches, the first two or three days are tedious beyond belief. The whole thing can — and often does — subside into a draw, a result generally satisfactory for the participants though frustrating for the spectators. But on rare occasions, beneath the seemingly calm surface, remarkable tension and excitement can be generated.

A case of this latter kind arose as the result of a dispute between two mood-music libraries. (Producers of films, television features and advertisements can rent from such a library — if they do not wish or cannot afford to commission original work — background music to fit any scene or situation imaginable.) It was the plaintiff's contention that whenever the defendants needed to fill a gap in their own collection, they simply hired a tape from one of their rivals and had it copied — with varying degrees of accuracy. One single recording owned by the plaintiff and allegedly pirated by the defendants was the actual subject of the action; but other recordings belonging to other firms which had been similarly treated had come into the plaintiff's possession. The defence was relying on the assertion that *their* version of the disputed tape had been made first; if, however, the judge were to hear several additional examples of obvious piracy this argument would cease to be credible, and the defendants would be placed in an impossible position. So for days a titanic battle between counsel was waged in court, the one side arguing that the additional tapes were admissible, the other — on the analogy of previous criminal convictions — that they were not. When the judge finally decided that it *was* in order for him to listen to all the tapes, the defence made the last desperate throw of challenging his ruling in the Court of Appeal. When that, too, failed they capitulated and agreed to settle on the plaintiff's terms. (Considering that one of the additional recordings was indistinguishable from Sibelius' *En Saga* — and was even described on the label, in a manner reminiscent of 'port-type' wine, as 'Saga-music' — they really had very little option.)

This clearly was a case, if it could be proved, of theft; comparable, perhaps, to the stealing of fashion designs in the rag-trade. As such it was exceptional; it can generally be assumed that copying has occurred subconsciously. As Michael Hurd has written in his book *The Composer* (OUP, 1968): 'From the moment (the composer) is born his mind begins to hoard each musical experience that comes his way. His mind, in fact, becomes a vast reference library of musical ideas, of which he may be only dimly aware.' There are well-attested examples of this in 'serious' music history. Alan Walker has traced the *Tristan* motif back to two songs: *Ich möchte hingehn* (written around 1845) and *Die Lorelei* (published in 1856):

Both were composed before *Tristan* was begun; and since the author was Wagner's father-in-law, Liszt, access can be taken as proved.

Recently a brief stir was caused by the claim that the opening motif of Elgar's *Enigma Variations* was derived from a phrase in Stanford's *Requiem*, which the composer is known to have played to Elgar on a visit to Malvern the previous year:

Although it is quite possible that this was the spark which ignited Elgar's imagination, no admirer of Stanford (and I am one) could possibly claim that these two bars were the source of a 'substantial part' of Elgar's masterpiece.

Parallels in contemporary literature come to mind. When in 1957 Christopher Isherwood came to re-issue his early novel *All the conspirators* he revealed the subconscious origin of some of the details: 'Speaking of Miss Durrant reminds me that there are two characters named Durrant AND a sailing scene off the Scilly Isles in Virginia Woolf's *Jacob's room*. This can't be mere coincidence. A psychic block, due perhaps to excessive reverence for Mrs Woolf, must have made me unconscious of my borrowings.' A bigger debt to a fellow writer was owed, on his own admission, by William Townend. In the 1930s he had an inspiration for a short story ('one of the few good ones I ever wrote') about the depredations of a giant rat. Some 20 years later, while in the process of editing *Performing Flea* ('a self-portrait in letters of PG Wodehouse'), he discovered that the plot was not after all his own invention, but had lain dormant in his subconscious ten years after being planted there by Wodehouse:

> 'Listen, Bill. Is this a crazy idea? I suddenly thought the other day, there are always rats on board ship, so why shouldn't one rat, starting by being a bit bigger than the others, gradually grow and grow, feeding on his little playmates, till he became the size of an Airedale terrier? Then there begin to be mysterious happenings on board the ship. Men are found dead with their faces chewed off, etc. And so on.
>
> 'Is this any good to you? It certainly isn't to me. I give it you with my blessing.'

Both these cases are clear-cut. Music is seldom quite so straightforward because it is made up of so many different elements (or parameters, to use the current jargon). Surprisingly perhaps where plagiarism is concerned, pitch may not be the most important of them. As Sullivan pointed out, we all have only eight notes at our disposal — or rather, since Schoenberg, twelve. An early song of mine, *My true love hath my heart*, begins with a short phrase which is identical — save for an unexpected cadence — with a theme from a piano piece by Chopin; so great, however, are all the other differences that this can hardly be anything but coincidence. More important than pitch are such things as mood, timbre and tempo — what might be generally summed up as the ambience of a composition. *Come scoglio*, from *Così fan tutte*, has scarcely a note in common with *Abscheulicher*, from *Fidelio*; but it is as certain as anything can be that Beethoven's portrait of Leonora (a heroic wife searching for her missing husband) is based on Mozart's portrait of Fiordiligi (a would-be heroic young woman planning to run away and join her fiancé who is abroad on active service.) That the arias of two such similar characters should both be set in the key of E major and feature an obbligato for French horn(s) cannot be explained in any other way.

Conscious borrowing is another thing again, and is strongly recommended by Vaughan Williams. Beethoven was the favourite source for what he provocatively termed his cribbing, although curiously enough Beethoven was not his favourite composer. (Equally curiously, *Così fan tutte* was not Beethoven's favourite Mozart opera.) The famous dissonance which introduces the finale of the 9th Symphony inspired the minor ninths which begin Vaughan Williams' No. 4, and Satan's dance in *Job* derives from the String Quartet op. 135 in F. The composer was surprised that no-one noticed these references, though he did not intend that the general public should immediately recognise them. With Charles Ives, on the other hand, we are in the realm of deliberately identifiable quotation; the first four notes of Beethoven's 5th Symphony are to be heard, in the *Concord* piano sonata, standing for all that is best in human aspiration.

To consider every debt owed to Beethoven by later composers would need a separate chapter. This might well begin with a consideration of the String Quartet op. 132 in A minor and its slow movement, the *Heiliger Dankgesang*, so ironically referred to by the dying Bartók in his last piano concerto and (less directly and less ironically) by the dying Britten in his last string quartet. Instead I would prefer to end with an example of a quotation taken from a very different composer and used in a very different medium: comic opera. Don Ferolo Whiskerandos, hero of Stanford's *The Critic, or an opera rehearsed*, has been run through in a duel with his arch-rival, the Beefeater. As he lies mortally wounded he sings these final words to the accompaniment of a familiar phrase from *Blest pair of sirens* on the orchestra:

> O cursed parry! — that last thrust in tierce
> Was fatal.

Epilogue
Is it possible that the plot which P G Wodehouse bequeathed to William Townend was itself subconsciously inspired by Sherlock Holmes' 'giant rat of Sumatra'?

19. Librettist malgré lui

My life-long love affair with the theatre began at the age of 12 when, for a holiday treat, one of my aunts invited me to a mid-week matinée. There was nothing on directly geared to my age-group, so my aunt chose as the likeliest offering a play which (to judge from its title) had a pleasantly rural setting and featured one of the favourite comedians of the day. She did, however, take the precaution of enquiring at the box-office whether it was likely to appeal to one of my tender years. On receiving the reply (a fair compromise between truth and the dictates of a commercial enterprise) 'Well, it is a *little* broad, madam', my aunt decided to risk it. We sat through about three-quarters of an hour of convoluted dialogue accompanied by much grotesque mopping and mowing. As the curtain fell on the first act my aunt, blushing bright scarlet, hustled me out of the theatre and took me to the nearest news cinema for a Mickey Mouse cartoon show.

I had understood less than nothing of what was taking place on the stage; but the episode left me with a firm conviction that there was something here which in the fulness of time would be worth enquiring into. The seed thus planted remained dormant for a few years, until it eventually blossomed into a devouring passion for all things theatrical. I did, however, retain a special affection for one particular branch of English drama — Restoration comedy; for the play to which my aunt had taken me was William Wycherley's *The Country Wife*.

For a musical boy theatre obviously included opera — particularly as Lancing College was only a tenor's throw from the recently opened Glyndebourne opera house. The tenor in question was Peter Pears. Being then at the start of his professional career he was just a rank-and-file member of the chorus; but because of his magnificent physique he was allowed one moment of stardom — in the non-singing rôle of King Duncan in Verdi's *Macbeth*. Through his agency two dress-rehearsal tickets for *Figaro* arrived at his old school, and I was the lucky recipient of one of them. From then on I looked at every play — whether set-book for the equivalent of O-levels, sixth-form Greek text, or the dramatic society's annual production — as potential operatic material. Lack of technique and opportunity relegated all these ideas to the category of day-dreams; but I stored them at the back of my mind for future use, much as a camel builds up its hump before setting out across the Sahara desert.

141

My first attempt to translate one of these dreams into reality was not a success. By way of a short cut I took an existing libretto (Sheridan's *The Duenna*), converted it into a one-acter by removing the sub-plot, and christened it *The Spanish Rivals*. Unfortunately the form used by Sheridan — songs linked by spoken dialogue — is an exceptionally difficult one for a novice, with no experience of dramatic pace and characterisation, to handle. So eventually I destroyed it, with the exception of the overture and a few songs which I left to sink or swim on their own.

One fringe benefit of *The Spanish Rivals* was that it brought me into contact with the Intimate Opera Company; and when they received an invitation to mount a week's season as part of the 1956 Cheltenham Festival this was just the stimulus I needed to try again — this time with a through-composed opera based on Molière's *Les Précieuses Ridicules*. I planned the scenario myself (under the title *If the cap fits*) without having any idea where the actual libretto was to come from. When Michael Tippett (so we are told) needed a librettist to complete his scenario for *A child of our time*, T S Eliot gave him so much encouragement that he went ahead and completed it himself. In the end I too was forced to do the same, though for precisely the opposite reason: nobody to whom I mentioned my idea showed the slightest interest in it whatsoever.

Molière's play concerns the come-uppance administered to two affected young ladies by their rejected suitors. I had already decided to take a hint from Boito and halve the number of principal characters. This was much to the liking of the Intimate Opera Company who (as their name suggests) favour small casts. To replace Molière's literary references with topical musical ones gave no difficulty. The hardest thing was providing rhymed verse for the set-pieces; where I already had a musical rhythm at the back of my mind the results were reasonably successful, less so when I had (so to speak) to pull myself up by my own bootlaces. I incorporated two visual recollections into the libretto. The final curtain, with the old father shaking his fist at the audience (on whose trendiness he blames his own predicament), derives from a memory of the original school production of the Molière in French in which I had taken part; and the revengeful suitor's parting burst of laughter was prompted by a similar treatment of the screen scene in an Oxford Playhouse production of Sheridan's *School for Scandal*.

At this time I had by no means resigned myself — as I did later — to becoming my own librettist in perpetuity; in fact for my next project, to be based on Stephen Vincent Benét's story *The devil and Daniel Webster*, I had discovered a drama colleague who was both able and willing to collaborate. Our plan fell through when the copyright owners declined to give permission for the use of the story. The only reason I can think of for their refusal (none was given) was that an American composer, Douglas Moore, had already written an opera on the same subject. It is a sobering thought that if this kind of protectionism had extended much further back into musical history we should have been obliged to dispense with Rossini's *Barber* and make do with Paisiello's. Another collaboration which disappointingly failed to materialise was with Eric Crozier. We had already begun to discuss plans for turning the legend of Caedmon into an opera when sudden and severe illness compelled him to withdraw.

This last blow came at a particularly awkward moment, as I had just been commissioned by Inglis Gundry to write a piece for the Sacred Music Drama Society. In desperation I turned to my camel's hump and called to mind a play which had long ago struck me as a possible operatic subject: John Drinkwater's $X = O$.

Re-reading Drinkwater's play, I was impressed all over again by the dramatic force and simplicity of the story-telling. In the original, the protagonists are two pairs of friends, besiegers and besieged, at the time of the Trojan War. In the first scenes we learn something of the essential goodness of their characters and the idealism of their motives. Impelled by the necessity of war, one of the Greeks and one of the Trojans make a sortie into enemy territory and succeed in killing the opponent who has been left behind. The final scenes of the play deal with their return and the discovery that in their absence death has solved the equation; and we are left with the realisation that war everywhere — whether it is waged at Troy or in Vietnam — always gives the same answer: X equals nothing.

A less skilful dramatist than Drinkwater might well have been defeated by the fact that much of the action calls of necessity for duplication (two killings, two discoveries). He surmounts this difficulty in masterly fashion. When the Greek comes back to camp after the raid, he recounts the details of his night's expedition quite unaware that his friend — seemingly just resting and quietly listening — is in fact dead. But the Trojan cannot return unaided; he needs his friend to lower the rope and haul him to safety up the city wall. All we see, therefore, in the final scene of the play is the dead soldier 'lying on the wall in the starlight and silence'; all we hear is the signal for the rope to be lowered, a signal which will never be answered.

When I started to adapt the text for operatic purposes, there arose a number of such formidable problems that I almost felt obliged to abandon the project. Not the least of these was the lack of variety —

in timbre (all four chief characters male, and no possible excuse for female voices anywhere in sight), and in character; for although Drinkwater had differentiated between the two pairs of friends, it was done by verbal means too subtle to survive transplanting into music. Then I remembered that the commissioning society proposed to perform the work in church, and though many religious people are now deeply concerned with the question of whether war is any longer (or ever was) an activity in which a Christian can (or could) in conscience participate, I doubted whether ordinary church-goers would see the relevance of a presentation of the siege of Troy. Lastly, although theoretically most subjects permit of many different treatments, no English composer in his senses could possibly contemplate a new opera set in Trojan times once having seen Tippett's overwhelming *King Priam*.

It was this last circumstance that gave me the vital clue, and I knew I was on the right track when I realised that in solving one problem I had in fact settled all the others simultaneously. Why not, I asked myself, change the place and period of the opera? Immediately the siege of Jerusalem (AD 70) by the Romans came into my mind, a siege that was actually foretold by Christ in his lifetime. A reading of Josephus' contemporary account of the siege enabled me to differentiate quite clearly between the Romans — givers of law and order, on their own Imperial terms — and the stubborn and fanatical members of the Jewish Resistance. Anything lacking for this purpose in Drinkwater's text was immediately supplied by phrases from the prophets and the psalms. A common feature of the siege was the attempted escape of non-combatants from the city through the Roman lines; in the early stages at any rate the lives of female prisoners were spared (at the price of slavery), which made the inclusion of a (small) chorus of Jewish women captured by the Romans not only possible but inevitable. Even the number of syllables involved (Greek-Trojan: Jew-Roman) seemed prearranged to ensure the minimum number of alterations to the original text. The only thing that did not occur to me, until after I had completed the opera, was the tragic topicality of the story in its new setting.

Some musical aspects of the work were dictated not by the libretto but by the circumstances of the commission. Since the performance was to take place in church, an organ was available; but because funds were low, only a limited number of other instruments could be added. Fortunately I had already experimented with an orchestra of ten soloists when executing an abortive commission* for incidental music to

---

* It was aborted by the Musicians Union, who (in pursuit of a vendetta with the British Council) blacked the recording.

144

The Merchant of Venice a short while previously; so to reinforce the organ I chose the same ensemble, consisting of four wind and four brass instruments, percussion and cello. The last-named was required to function as a complete string section on its own — in the more lyrical moments acting as a second 'voice' in duet with one of the characters on stage, at others supplying the bass of the ensemble. I tried to emulate Drinkwater in treating parallel events in different ways. The Jewish sentry (in civilian life a musician) is attacked while singing a song he has himself composed, and the struggle takes place against a deliberately formal march played by the complete instrumental ensemble; the scene of the killing of the Roman officer is entirely wordless, and is accompanied by a series of diminishing rhythmic patterns on a single kettledrum. The over-all confrontation is represented by a clash of two keys, C sharp minor and D minor. This is heard in its most uncompromising form in the opening music given to the chorus of prisoners. It recurs at climactic points in the opera and (like the dramatic situation itself) remains unresolved at the end. Incidentally, this clash of two keys a semitone apart was the basic musical idea which had come to me when I first thought of Drinkwater's play as potential operatic material many years before.

Meanwhile, a performance of *If the cap fits* by students of the Guildhall School of Music and Drama led to the commissioning of a new piece to be written specially for them. This time my subconscious suggested the subject in a curiously roundabout way. I began by dreaming that I had set to music Oscar Wilde's *The Importance of being Ernest*; this — since the play relies for its effect far more on dialogue than on situation and character — was obviously an impossible choice. However, it did remind me of one of Wilde's short stories which I had once heard very effectively dramatised on the radio. *Lord Arthur Savile's crime* is the tale of a nobleman who has the misfortune to be told by a palmist on the eve of his wedding that he is destined to commit a murder. As a man of integrity, Lord Arthur naturally conceives it to be his duty to get the murder over and done with before settling down to the responsibilities of family life ... But *The Importance of being Ernest* was not totally abandoned; I borrowed from it two epigrams about music, two names (Lane and Merriman) for the servants and — much the most important — the domineering characteristics of Lady Bracknell. (I gave these to the Duchess of Paisley, whose original amiable woolliness struck me as unbecoming to a contralto.) All that remained to be done to make the story viable as an opera was to avoid duplication by showing only one of Lord Arthur's murderous failures on stage, while simply referring to the other in passing. By this means I was able to keep the number of scenes to three: an evening party in Lady Windermere's house, the shop of a well-known anarchist in Soho where Lord Arthur goes to purchase some high explosive, and the Victoria Embankment, EC4 (then, by a happy coincidence, the address of the Guildhall School which had commissioned the opera).

I found plenty of vivid dialogue in the story which could be transferred to the stage without alteration. I wanted there to be a Victorian ballad sung at the party in scene one by Lord Arthur's fiancée; failing to unearth anything suitable in Wilde, I found just what I needed among the poems of one of his contemporaries, Dollie Radford. The other set-pieces are based on Wilde's own words, re-assembled as necessary to fit the appropriate context. The anarchist's catalogue of his wares in scene two, for instance (including the explosive clock which Lord Arthur ultimately chooses, and a booby-trapped umbrella), is compiled from items mentioned on four quite separate occasions. The list is presented in a series of rhymed couplets of unequal length which, doggerel though they are, give exactly the right flexibility needed for the contemporary equivalent of a *buffo* aria:

> Next, for a treat —
> It's really something rather neat —
> A meteorological thermometer,
> Or some would say, barometer.
> Touch it when the dial reads warm and dry
> And you'll be blown — pouf! — sky high.

The last line, with its onomatopoeic explosion, embodies yet another visual memory. The French husband of a friend with whom my wife and I often stay in Paris had recently had an electrifying experience while trying to repair the wiring of his car. The Gallic gestures and ejaculations with which he illustrated his account of the episode seemed tailor-made for my excitable (but ineffective) anarchist.

Similarly in scene three, the love-duet draws on the splendid descriptive passages with which the story abounds, linked together by the recurring phrase 'How beautiful London is when you're in love'. This can be justified (if justification is needed) by the fact that Wilde himself used to convert such descriptive passages into poems when it suited his purpose. Here is the River Thames at night, as seen by Lord Arthur Savile:

> How unreal everything looked! How like a strange dream! The houses on the other side of the river seemed built out of darkness ... The huge dome of St. Paul's loomed like a bubble through the dusky air.

146

Inspired perhaps by the Nocturnes of his friend and enemy, the painter Whistler, Wilde later turned the passage into verse:

> The yellow fog came creeping down
> The bridges, till the houses' walls
> Seemed changed to shadows, and St. Paul's
> Loomed like a bubble o'er the town.

As with *The Equation*, a number of musical decisions were taken out of my hands. I needed the traditional type of orchestra for *Lord Arthur*, but as the pit would hold only 30 players I dispensed with one section of violins and included a piano. The stage was too small for a chorus, so in the party scene I used instead an ensemble of soloists. (There would be no objection to employing 'extras' as a chorus of guests if the opera were to be produced in a bigger theatre.) It is the great blessing — and curse — of writing opera that creative ideas flow easily only when the composer is forced to cope with a particular set of theatrical circumstances. (On a much loftier plane, this was Mozart's experience in Munich when he discovered the technical deficiencies of the singers for whom he was contracted to write *Idomeneo*.) Opera composition *in vacuo* is a near impossibility.

The perfect illustration of this was provided by my latest stage work, *The cat who went to heaven*. Its form — a music-theatre piece with equal opportunities for actors, dancers, singers and players — was dictated entirely by the place (Westonbirt School) and the people (London University extra-mural students) for whom it was written. It took advantage of the presence among us of a drama producer, a choreographer and a specialist in stage design. The component parts had to be kept fairly separate, so that simultaneous rehearsals could be held during the five afternoons which were all that were available for preparation. Our sole instrumental resources were piano duet, percussion, and a small chamber organ which stood at one end of the school hall. (For a subsequent performance in London I prepared an alternative score for an instrumental ensemble of 11 players.)

The action, which takes place 'once upon a time, far away in China', begins with a musical prologue. The chorus, led by two monks, pronounce the traditional Buddhist curse on the only animal which dared to rebel against the Buddha. Actors take over as the scene shifts to the house of a poor young painter, whose housekeeper has just spent most of their last remaining pennies not on dinner but on — a cat. The artist's anger is dispelled by the cat's lucky markings, her good manners, her gentleness, and (not least) her piety; every day she joins him at his prayers before the image of the Buddha on its low shelf.

147

Some little time after the arrival of Good Fortune (as she has been named) the artist is chosen by lot to paint a picture of the death of the Buddha for the neighbouring temple. (Was this pure chance, or could it be that the Buddha would listen to the prayers of a little spotted cat?) While the artist works on the picture it is the turn of the dancers, who mime the story of three of the Buddha's incarnations. The painting — which is to represent the Buddha lying still with his arms at his side while the gods, the disciples, and all the animals with one exception come to say goodbye to him — gradually nears completion; but Good Fortune becomes progressively more and more unhappy as still no sign of a cat appears among the leave-takers. At last the artist can bear her misery no longer; though fully aware that it was forbidden he takes up his best brush and 'last of all the animals — drew *a cat.*' Whereupon Good Fortune falls dead, too happy to live another minute.

Next day the Abbot comes from the temple to see the painting and, finding it to be heretical, takes it away to be burnt. The artist is ruined, but *he doesn't care*; while painting the story of the Buddha he has learnt the meaning of self-sacrifice. At dawn he is roused from his thoughts by the approach of a triumphant procession, singing, shouting and letting off fireworks; at its head is the Abbot, carrying his picture. There has been a miracle; Good Fortune is no longer last of all the animals but the first, and the Buddha's left arm is no longer at his side but stretched out over her in blessing.

Preparing a libretto from Elizabeth Coatsworth's story did not prove too difficult a problem. Besides containing some very serviceable dialogue for the actors, each chapter was prefaced by a lyric which needed little if any adaptation in order to become the text for the singers. Much thought had to be given, however, to the representation of Good Fortune the cat. In the end it seemed best to let her remain imaginary, and to instruct the actors to conjure up her existence in the minds of the audience by their own gestures and expressions. She does, of course, appear in person on the 'miracle' painting which the Abbot displays to the audience during the final tableau; there could be no better model for this than the drawings made by Kiddell-Munroe for Elizabeth Coatsworth's original book.

Postscript

Chapter 1: The Geoffrey Bush works played and recorded (see page 11) were the Divertimento for strings; Trio for oboe, bassoon and piano; and *Dialogue* for oboe and piano.

Chapter 6: The editions of the Purcell Society are published by Novello.

Chapter 9: R J S Stevens' *It was a lover and his lass* and the catches by Arne, Calcott, Horsley, Paxton and Webbe are published in the series *Invitation to the Partsong* (Stainer and Bell). It is intended to include Spofforth's glee *Blest pair of sirens* and the madrigals by Beale, Horsley, Linley and Pearsall in later volumes of the same series.

Chapter 10: Sterndale Bennett's *Suite de pièces* and the Piano Sonata No 1 in F minor are published in Musica Britannica, volume 37. The suite is also available separately as an off-print (Stainer and Bell).

Chapter 11: The Parry songs discussed in this chapter are published in *Musica Britannica*, volume 49. The Stanford songs will be published in a later volume in the same series.

Chapter 14: Balfour Gardiner's *Comedy Overture, News from Whydah* and *Shepherd Fennel's dance* are obtainable on hire from Novello.

Chapter 15: The complete songs and solo piano music of John Ireland are published by Stainer and Bell. All Ireland's major works are available on Lyrita records. Chandos have issued a 2-record set of piano music, entitled *John Ireland, his friends and pupils* (DBRD 2006).

Chapter 17: Geoffrey Bush's songs are published by Novello with the exception of the following: *A little love music* (Basil Ramsey), *Greek love songs* (Stainer and Bell) and *The end of love* (Stainer and Bell). These three, together with the *Songs of Wonder* and the *Three songs of Ben Jonson*, are recorded on Chandos ABRD 1053. Symphony No 1 is published (study score) by Novello and recorded on Lyrita SRCS 115.

Chapter 19: Geoffrey Bush's opera *If the cap fits* is published by Stainer and Bell; *The Equation* and *Lord Arthur Savile's crime* by Novello; and *The cat who went to heaven* by Basil Ramsey.

*   *   *

A discography of Geoffrey Bush's music can be obtained from the British Institute of Recorded Sound, 29 Exhibition Road, London SW7. The BIRS offers a free playback service to any member of the public. Scores and tapes can also be seen and heard at the British Music Information Centre, 10 Stratford Place, London, W1.

*   *   *

In some of the chapters of this book use is made of material which in its original form first appeared in *Composer, The Listener, Musica Britannica, Performing Right, Proceedings of the Royal Musical Association, Recorded Sound, Records and Recording,* and *The Times.* All of it has, however, been either revised or rewritten expressly for this book. The author is grateful to the owners for permission to use such sections as are still copyright.

Index

Entries for the works of Geoffrey Bush are made under the titles of those works; entries for the music of all other composers and writers are made under the name of the person indexed.